TRUE LOVE KNOT

entangled ~ a caregiver's story

The KNOT Series gives a voice to modern social issues that are frequently hushed. The novels untangle struggles and interlock relationships as the characters heal and achieve happiness.

TRUE LOVE KNOT

entangled ~ a caregiver's story

DonnaLee OVERLY

TRUE LOVE KNOT
Copyright © 2021 by DonnaLee Overly

For permission, please contact the author at www.donnaleeoverly.com or e-mail donnaleeoverly@gmail.com.

Printed in the United States of America

First Edition, October 2021

Fernandina Beach, Florida

Cover and Interior design by Roseanna White Designs
True Love Knot artwork by DonnaLee Overly

Library of Congress Control Number: 2021915375
ISBN Trade Paperwork- 13: 978-1-7352517-2-1
E-BOOK: 13: 978-1-7352517-3-8

www.donnaleeoverly.com

This book is dedicated to the caregivers —
true heroes who work tirelessly and generously
give of themselves.

"*There are only four kinds of people in the world:*
Those who have been **caregivers**.
Those who are currently **caregivers**.
Those who will be **caregivers**,
and those who will need a **caregiver**."
~ Rosalyn Carter

"*Everyone, is of course free to interpret the work in his own way.*
I think seeing a picture is one thing and interpreting it is another. "
~ Jasper Johns

CHAPTER 1

His body shakes as the thunder roars. She reaches for his hand, and her thumb rubs against an old callous. This one, on his left thumb, was rightfully earned after years of swinging a tennis racquet and working on her daddy's cattle ranch.

"It's just the wind blowing through the trees. Some branches must be hitting the roof." Her tone is calm, just the opposite of her inner turmoil. It's not the sixty-plus mile per hour winds nor the torrents of rain that cause her angst; instead, it is rooted in the endless waiting and vanishing hope now dangling by tattered threads. It's a different sort of storm from the one currently howling outside, but a storm, nonetheless.

She twirls the band on his ring finger. Tomorrow is a milestone. Yes, it's been four months since his accident, and she curses the question that pops into her mind more frequently with each passing day that she witnesses his lifeless body. Would he have been better off dying?

This question buzzes in her mind like a pesky fly, and no amount of shooing makes it go away. If she answers truthfully, she'll label the woman staring back from the mirror a terrible wife, and the door of guilt that's already begging to be opened will welcome self-condemnation. She closes her eyes. She's only human. Is she naïve to hope that others could understand?

For now, learning how to cope is the only question that demands a reply, one that she controls. She remembers that first week, one that was full of promise. Brett had fallen from a bull and was trampled. He was young and vibrant and had always conquered whatever hurdle was before him. She trusted he would get through this, despite what the doctors said.

With downcast eyes, she bites her upper lip before looking up to study his face. She believes he's in there somewhere because, at times, his emerald eyes seem to follow her. His body is damaged, but is his soul? No one can say for sure. The brain scan was inconclusive, and a subsequent test showed no improvement.

He's in there, my Brett, the man I love with all my heart. Telepathy isn't proven, but can he read my thoughts? She's fearful that he can sense her anxiety. She covers her face with her hands. Would her burden lighten if she gave voice to her fears? His nonverbal response to her appalling confession might provide insight into his condition. Is she brave enough to share?

Just now, his body jerks after the flash of lightning, followed by the roar of thunder and another noise hitting the roof. Her longing that he may be aware is supported, and it pains her to revisit their past, a time when she unconsciously took his words and touch for granted. She misses his strong, muscular body and his deep dimple that flaunted mischievous behavior. Eight months ago, they said their vows. This was not their plan.

Please, please, come back. We're too young to live this way—a feeding tube, ventilator, suction machine, diapers, and a Geri chair. These words had been absent from her vocabulary before his accident, and now she says them numerous times daily. She's learned many new words, most of them medical jargon, due to his complex injuries. She has learned about neuromuscular blocking agents and polyneuropathy because, in addition to the scans that confirm brain damage, the cervical fractures are responsible for the paralysis—a double dose of bad luck.

Closing her eyes, she offers another prayer, although she's losing hope. Lately, it seems like as the wind outside scatters debris, her mound of unanswered prayers for improvements in her husband's health flees, taking away her faith. *How can God be so mean? How can I make restitution? We need a miracle. God, are you listening?*

At times like this, her self-doubt creeps in like an insidious termite, gnawing away from the inside out. It must be because of her wavering belief, for if her faith were firm, God would have intervened, right? Is she being punished? She has gone to her knees and cried, begging for a sign.

Once, she was so broken that she collapsed from sheer exhaustion. The nurses found her on the floor the next morning and helped her to bed. Still, no miracles; it's the same, day after day, week after week, and month after month.

Gabby's the only daughter of the cattle rancher and oil baron, Wayne King. With all his influential friends and money, even he hasn't been able to fix this mess. In the past, she would cry and pout, or better yet, bake him chocolate-chip cookies, and these acts were sure to melt his heart. And then later, his reflection shining in her eyes, this was all the reward he needed. These requests weren't always selfish because many good things had come from her asking, such as the recently founded Equine Assisted Therapy Center. And unaware to her and more times than her daddy had fingers, he had made the rough paths under her feet smooth; however, those stories are for another day.

Brett, you really did it this time. Her head lowers from the weight of the unfortunate event, his foolish decision that started this nightmare.

Due to the earlier storm predictions, she dismissed the regular nurse. Gabby didn't want the young woman to travel the long drive home in dangerous conditions. She can handle Brett's care. Months ago, she started learning one step at a time by asking the nurses to explain as they performed their duties. Her goal was to become his primary caregiver, and within a few weeks, she was willing and able.

Physically, it takes all her strength to roll him over, bathe him, and provide fresh linens, but she's young and strong-willed. And she's his wife. However, mentally that's a horse of a different color.

Being angry with God isn't helping. Instead of coming to terms with fate, she has clicked through the first four stages of the grieving process: denial, anger, bargaining, and depression. Somehow the last stage, the acceptance stage, never comes as she reverts to anger, and it's where she's presently stuck. She's angry with God and Brett, but more so, she's angry at herself.

During these last two months, she's left many household duties undone because she has devoted all of her energy and time to her husband's care. Even when the nurses work their shift to give her a break, she's reluctant to leave his side. She is desperate for any minute sign of improvement, from completing his essential daily activities to endless hours sitting by his bedside, watching each breath and straining to see the slightest movement in a finger or toe.

She recalls her excitement just a few days after the accident when his index finger gave the tiniest twitch, that first indication of recovery. However, no further signs have appeared, almost to the point where she now questions if it was an illusion because she wished it so desperately. Then, days later, without any other movement, the doctors dismissed her observation as an involuntary reflex. She continued to hold vigil for weeks to prove them wrong. The nurses would lower their heads and offer no encouragement. With her previous overwhelming joy vanishing, the last thing she needed was their pity.

In her weariness, she sank lower than ever, and during this time, when all hope seemed to have faded, she was unexpectedly offered a brief escape. Now, thinking about it, goose bumps rise on her arms, and she shudders. How could she have done this? Often, caregivers are described as angels on earth. She has fought to live this role for her husband, but she fell from grace when she accepted the offer. Much like the angel Lucifer, who, as his punishment, God cast out of heaven.

She pinches her upper lip, allowing a lone tear to drop off her chin as she rubs his callous. *Can he feel my touch? Is he aware of my sin?* Her head rests on his arm, and her blond hair covers his chest as another streak of lightning brightens the night sky. With care, she slides into his warm bed, wrapping his arm over her shoulder. It's at night, cuddled next to him, when she pretends to resume their lives as newlyweds and hopes that her dreams will continue the happier times.

This same evening, Wayne and Rita King, Rusty, the ranch fore-man, and Jamie, his wife, the housekeeper and cook, are gathering for dinner. As King washes his hands at the sink, he looks to his wife. He knows the answer before he asks. The house feels cold, void of chatter and laughter, the companions his daughter usually brings with her. However, that was before the accident.

"She didn't come, did she?"

Rita looks at her husband with sadness. "No, she declined again. This is the fifth, maybe sixth, time in a row. I've lost track. Do you think we should go over there?"

He diligently scrubs his hands. "Maybe...something needs to change. The nurse reports that she's up all hours of the night. They also report that she's more critical. The evening nurse forgot the small pillow for under his wrist, and Gabby screamed. The poor girl was so shaken, she refused to come back the next day. That's just not like Gabby."

"I'm worried, Wayne. We all are." She looks at Rusty and Jamie.

Jamie nods. "I even made her favorite chips—fried sweet pota-toes—hoping the wind would blow that smell right to their house and entice her over." Jamie wipes her hands on her apron. "She's never stayed away this long. Not since I can remember, and that goes back quite a few years, mind you." She waves her spatula in King's direc-tion. "But it's supposed to storm again later tonight, so maybe that's why she didn't come."

King looks out the window at his daughter's house across the field. She had it built on the acres he gifted her this past year. As a child, she loved to catch crawdads in the stream, swim, and fish in the lake. Now, both serve as the view from her front porch. He can see her house lights through the grove of oak trees, and he runs his fingers through his full head of white hair. Parents never cease to worry about their children, even when they're grown. Under these unusual circumstances, maybe he should take matters into his own hands. It's not good for her to carry this burden alone.

CHAPTER 2

Four Months Earlier, February

The rodeo tour had started again in the small town of Kingston as it does each spring. After the cows and their calves are moved to the spring pastures, the rodeo fever starts spreading. The previous year, Brett had placed second in the National Rodeo event in Vegas. The entire King family made the trip: Gabby, her daddy and his wife Rita, and her stepbrother, Stan. They flew on the King's private jet, but Rusty, the ranch foreman, and Brett drove the truck that trailered the horses because they had wanted to arrive early and watch some of the other rodeo events. Their family had a grand time celebrating in the city that never sleeps. Brett came away proudly sporting a second-place belt for the calf tie-down. It was a joyous crowning moment.

Late this afternoon, with the completion of the chores that included moving the cattle from the winter pastures to the summer pasture, the hired hands wished to reward themselves. So, with local talk about the rodeo tour starting again, they decided some friendly competition would be good practice. At first, they roped calves until one of the ranch hands thought it would be fun to try their hand at bull riding. One particular bull from that winter's stockyard auction had been giving the wranglers problems for weeks now.

"That's the meanest bull I've ever seen," Rusty, the ranch foreman of two decades on the King Ranch and a longtime friend of Wayne King, says as he points to a large black and brown bull that the men have driven into the corral.

"How so?" Brett, Gabby's husband, asks as he leans his muscular frame on the corral fence, chewing a blade of grass. He removes his Stetson and wipes the sweat from his brow before running his hand through his brown curls.

"I can see it in his eyes. He's got the devil in him."

"Really? Maybe he's mad that his freedom has been stolen. And now, he's a bit claustrophobic. He's used to wide open spaces and being the boss. If I were that bull, I'd be agitated too."

The two men watch as the wranglers rope the bull and pull him into the gate. The bull bucks and resists, but after some struggle, they manage.

"This will be interesting," says Rusty, rubbing his chin.

One of the young ranch hands volunteers to ride first. Bets are on, and the hat is passed around. Can Junior pull this off? A typical ride is eight seconds.

"I give him two seconds." The older man shakes his head. "Young and foolish, but he's got balls."

Junior's face is tight, and his teeth are clenched as the gate is opened and the bull runs loose, bucking and stamping. The ride is brief, and timing it at two seconds is being generous.

"I told you he was mean, aww… it's more than that. He's got the Oklahoma temperament." Rusty rubs his chin. "Mark my words, he's got that Plummer trait. Just watch him—the way he rolled to the side just now with Junior on his back. That right there is what they call sun fishing… when his feet come off the ground. He's a mean one, all right. We should name him Grinch."

"Grinch, I like that." Brett replaces his Stetson and joins in clapping and shouting words of encouragement for the next brave rider. He turns back to face Rusty. "They worked hard these past few days. It's nice to see the men having fun." He reaches for more bills from his wallet to add to the hat. "It's good, clean fun."

"It's dangerous fun. They don't know anything about bull riding. You've got to keep your back straight and lean forward. That's the key. Lean forward and keep to the bull's shoulder."

"How do you know this?"

"There's a lot I could tell you, youngins." The older man chuckles, turns, then walks away.

Gabby's working at the horse center when her phone rings.

"Gabby, Brett's had…there's been an accident. They… the medics took him to the hospital…by helicopter." Rita, her stepmother, is talking fast, and Gabby needs to concentrate on getting the full meaning of the jumbled phrases.

"What happened to Brett?"

"He was bull riding and got trampled."

"Bull riding? He doesn't do that. How did this happen?"

"The men at the ranch were practicing for the rodeo, and Brett gave it a try. I'm sorry, honey, that's all I know. It's not good."

"Okay, okay." Her mind is racing.

"Your dad is on his way to pick you up. Stan and Marie can cover the center. He should be there in another five minutes or so."

At the hospital, Gabby and her daddy wait outside the surgical wing's automatic doors. Dr. James enters.

"Mr. King, Ms. Matthews, they're getting Brett settled in intensive care, then you can see him. We fit him with a halo vest that will stabilize his cervical spine, which has pins inserted into his skull. Though this can be pretty intimidating, I assure you that it doesn't hurt. It looks like this." Dr. James hands Gabby a brochure. "There's a lot of swelling, and the x-rays indicate a fractured fourth and fifth cervical vertebrae. In addition to the fractures, the CT shows torn tissue and bleeding in the brain. We won't know the full extent of the damage until some of the swelling goes down. He's receiving intravenous meds to help with that. He's comatose, and at this time, that's for the best. If he weren't, we'd induce a coma so that his body can rest. Rest is the best thing for him."

"How long will it take for the swelling to go down? He'll wake up then, right?" Gabby searches the doctor's face for an encouraging sign.

"With cases this severe, I really can't say."

"Severe? So, it's really bad?"

He nods. "The large amount of bleeding in the brain and tissue tearing makes this critical."

"Oh no." Her knees buckle.

King wraps his arms around his daughter.

"Hey, it's too soon to tell. He's young and strong. Give him a chance," King says with confidence.

Dr. James puts his clipboard under his arm. "He's on a ventilator. The tube goes through his vocal cords, so even if he were awake, he'd be unable to speak. If you don't have any more questions, I'll check in on him again and tell the nurses to come to get you."

King says, "Thank you so much. We know that Brett will be in good hands."

Dr. James says, "We'll keep him sedated tonight. After you see him, I advise that you go home, get some rest, and come back in the morning. We'll call you if there are any changes during the night."

King nods. Gabby raises her head briefly to meet the doctor's eyes, expecting a sign of optimism. In them, her promise to find hope shatters because all they express is, "I'm sorry."

CHAPTER 3

March

Gabby kisses Brett on the forehead, then strokes his hair. "It's a big day today. I'm taking you home. You've been here four weeks, and that's four weeks too long. You and I get to ride in an ambulance. I'm going with you; make sure you'll be safe."

She turns to the windows. "It's sunny outside—a good day for a ride through the hill country. Having some sun on your face will be a good thing. I know you miss it." She turns back to the bed. "I got the house ready. The rec room with the big fireplace will be your temporary bedroom—lots of sunlight from the big windows. There's plenty of space for all of your stuff and the nursing staff. Yes, Daddy insisted that you have only the best care, so we hired nursing staff twenty-four/seven. You'll do better in our home, and we'll both be happier. I've had enough of this hospital room, especially that overhead speaker. I jump whenever an announcement comes through."

She sits on the bed and holds his hand. "At home, we'll have some time alone. I miss us, Brett. Please open your eyes. Squeeze my hand, anything to let me know that you're in there." There's no response.

"Knock, knock."

She turns to face the door.

"Oh, hi, Daddy… Rita. We're still waiting for transport. They were supposed to be here ten minutes ago."

King leans down to kiss his daughter. "They're here at the nurse's station, filling out paperwork."

"Great, we'll soon be on our way."

King flips his Stetson back and forth between his hands. "You sure about this?"

"I don't understand. Explain."

"Taking him to the ranch, away from the immediate care that's available here. What if something happens?" His eyes find his daughter's.

"That's why we're hiring nurses, right? They're trained to handle situations. It's not like he's going to stop breathing. He's already intubated."

"Honey, I want to be certain that you're fully aware of what you're undertaking here. It's a huge responsibility."

"I want my husband back in our home. He's here in this sterile…"

The overhead speakers interrupt, announcing, "…Medical alert… room 2108…Medical alert…room 2108…Medical alert room 2108."

She cups her hands over her ears, then stands and yells, "It makes me want to scream."

King and Rita share concerned looks. It seems that Gabby's as stressed emotionally as her husband is compromised physically.

"I want my husband home, in our house. I want us to be as normal as we can. We have no privacy. I can't even sleep next to him. You come and go, stay away days at a time. I'm here every day. I know what goes on. I never know which nurse is working. I have to give instruction continually. He likes this, and please don't do that. I should be hoarse from repeatedly telling them that he needs to lie on his side after giving him a tube feeding. They should know that." She rubs her forehead. "It'll be safer for him at home. I'll have more control. We'll get more consistent staffing who will know the routine, making my life easier." She throws her hands in the air. "I thought you were supportive. I never imagined I would have to fight you." She sits and hangs her head. "You have no idea," she sobs.

"Oh, Princess, you're right. We haven't been here every day. We don't know Brett's routine. I didn't think of it that way. I'm sorry." He kneels in front of her. "I'm sorry, so sorry. I had no idea." He hugs her. "Let's get our boy home. Okay?"

She gazes up with watery eyes and nods. "It needs to be different. It needs to change. I can't do this anymore. I need my husband home."

King hugs her again and raises his worried eyes to his wife.

The ambulance ride is uneventful, and the nurses get Brett settled with ease into the Matthews' residence. The sun shines through the large windows, and Gabby holds her shoulders back with a smile gracing her face. She has accomplished the first step on her path to getting her life as close to normal as possible.

Now that her husband's back home, she'll implement the rest of her plan. Over the past four weeks, she's closely observed the nurses' duties. She's even helped with Brett's care. She's learned about administering the tube feedings, care for the Foley catheter, and how to give a bed bath. She learned how to use a tray to shampoo his hair. True, the ventilator and the tracheal tube suctioning scare her, but she'll learn. She knows she can do this. She must.

With each day, she continues to learn the tiny steps to get to her goal—to cuddle and sleep next to him as husband and wife. She'll be his caregiver, the ultimate display of love. She wants to be alone with him because when they're alone, lying next to each other, she can close her eyes and pretend. That is magical. It rids the feeling of being cold, a feeling that every organ in her body has stopped functioning correctly.

After these weeks in the hospital with the many blood tests and scans, her heart aches. The results have shown no improvements. In fact, they have leaned in the opposite direction. She doesn't deny these changes. Instead, she continues to pray daily for a miracle, an intervention from God to change their circumstances. She wishes to have a different outcome.

CHAPTER 4

May

Gabby wipes her brow. She wonders if Brett has gained weight because it takes more strength to roll him over. She presses her fingers into his ankles. The indentations leave finger marks, so she presses farther up his calf, finding similar results. Her eyes follow the catheter tube to the dark-amber urine full of sediment in the reservoir bag. Does he have another urinary infection, or does this fluid retention indicate kidney shutdown? Perhaps this is a newly developing problem for her to research.

She lowers her head from the weight of one more complication that's plagued them since bringing him home. Taking him out of the hospital was a noble idea; she suffers no regret. Their lives may never be normal again, but she'll take this to the alternative that was certain to steal her sanity.

She convinces herself that these problems will exist regardless of his location. It's inevitable as his condition continues to deteriorate.

Exhausted from reading countless medical journals with the newest research findings, she still holds on to hope, but it's hanging on a tattered thread. She turns to jot a note on the whiteboard, communicating this new concern to the nurse who will arrive for the morning shift.

She strokes Brett's freshly washed hair. "Hey, sexy, you smell good." She wraps a curl around her finger. A few days ago, she caught one of the evening nurses with scissors, ready to snip his brown locks. Yes, she went off like a crazy person, scaring the nurse almost to death. Gabby felt bad when the woman cried and apologized before running from the room, hiding her river of tears. She'll never cut his hair. It growing is a reminder that he's alive.

During the day, she's positioned him to face the window, and she speaks to him as if he can understand. One day, she prays, he'll answer. As her words float around the room, it's probably more therapy for her than help to her husband. She tells him bits and pieces of their life story. At times, she laughs out loud at the joys and then cries equally as hard for the heartaches. While telling stories, she rubs his feet and massages his legs, which also provides physical therapy. She is careful to follow her notes made from watching the movements and manipulations the therapists use. Usually, during the evenings, she'll read Western romance novels aloud, believing that hearing her words about herding cattle and riding on horseback combined with romance will remind him of their special love story and jar him from his slumber.

A few weeks after moving him home and becoming competent with the monstrous ventilator and tracheal tube suctioning, she started dismissing the night nurse. She is finally free to crawl into his bed, snuggle up and position his arm around her shoulders. For the first time in a little over a month, she doesn't feel alone in the fight. She breathes in his aftershave and takes comfort, feeling warm and secure.

The morning after, she thinks they both slept better than they had since his accident. Not once did he seize or jerk. She senses that he's aware of her presence. This was her goal: get him home, surround him with gentle clues to permeate his psyche, and with hope and prayers, coax him out of his deep sleep.

Sitting in the hospital day after day and night after night, she knew that there had to be a better way, and tonight lying beside him, she closes her eyes as a tear slides down her cheek. She loves this man more than life itself and prays for the miracle that will bring him back, sure that his accident can be reversed.

Nestled in the crux of his arm, she dreams of a time when their love was new.

They had just finished horseback riding and were leading Frog and Lady along the path next to the lake. The sun rays streamed through the oak trees' branches, and the birds flitted from one tree to another with their cheery songs.

"This is my favorite spot on the ranch." She gazed into his green eyes.

"And why is that?"

"I love the sound of the creek and watching the birds fly over the lake. If I'm lucky, I get to see them dive down and skim just over the water. Sometimes the bees will get a drink, and of course, there is always the chance of a fish jumping or a hummingbird sipping nectar from the plants along the water's edge. It's a touch of heaven here on the ranch." She turned and opened her arms wide, pointing toward the meadow across the way. "Someday, I'm going to build a house right here."

"That sounds nice." He reached for her chin and lifted her face,

searching her eyes. With a seriousness that she didn't think he was capable of, he asked, "Any possibility that I can live here in heaven with you?"

She giggled. "Is this a marriage proposal?"

"That's presumptuous. I was asking about the opportunity to be your stable boy." His eyes danced, and his dimple deepened.

"Oh, the rumors I've heard about those stable boys and what goes on. That could be interesting." Her face turned a slight shade of red.

"Ms. King, it sounds like you're willing to give me a chance. At least a job interview." He pulled her close.

Their eyes locked, and he pressed his lips to hers. His tongue was gentle and teasing when she pulled away. But clearly not finished, he reached for her lips again, and she got lost as though under his spell.

She wakes to the sound of the ventilator beeping. The gurgling noise indicates that Brett needs suctioning to clear the mucus from the narrow tube. Reluctantly, she lifts the covers and slides out from her warm nest into the chilled room. As she glances out the window, she sees the bright glow in the east, hinting that the sun will soon grace the horizon to start another day. *She remembers her dream and says a prayer of gratitude that she and her love were together once again last night.* Her shoulders fill with tension as she turns on the suction machine and unwraps a catheter.

"Ms. Matthews, good morning," a voice calls from the far side of the room.

"Oh, Liz, I didn't hear you come in. You're early." She wraps her arms around herself, aware of the thin nightgown showing the silhouette of her body as she addresses the middle-aged nurse.

Liz has turned, already heading for the kitchen. "I'll make us some coffee and warm Mr. Matthew's tube feeding."

Liz is a good soul, her favorite nurse because she anticipates Brett's needs and always has a kind word. The two women have forged a friendship, so Gabby trusts her with the keys to the front door. As they have spent time caring for Brett, they have discovered common interests. Liz speaks of things that are frequently on Gabby's mind but would never say.

"Liz, you're Brett's favorite nurse."

"Thank you, Ms. Matthews. That's nice of you to say."

"I say it because it's true. You know exactly what he needs. He seems to rest better in your care. I've grown to trust you, and I know that my husband does too." She helps Liz turn Brett to change the sheets. "Have you always been a nurse?"

"Heavens no, child. My late husband had cancer. It was advanced when he was diagnosed because he wasn't one to go to a doctor. He thought if he ignored the pain, it would eventually go away. We were both surprised by the news that he was given only six months to live." Liz tucks the clean sheets under Brett's back.

"I'm sorry," she says as she rolls Brett back the other way and pulls the clean sheet through.

"Like you, I didn't want him in a nursing home or hospice. I wanted him home, and he felt the same. If I had to do it over again, I wouldn't change a thing. Some folks don't get it."

"Don't get what?"

"Get that you aren't just doing it for the person who is dying, but you're also doing it for you."

Their eyes met, and in a brief second, an untold story unfolded.

Liz ends the conversation by saying, "When I care for Brett, I feel close to Rob."

At first, when the nurse spoke of her own husband's demise, it made Gabby uncomfortable. However, since that conversation, Gabby has read the love in the spaces between the words. Liz's stories hold nuggets of wisdom. Gabby never tires of hearing them, and when they are stories that put a smile on her face, she imagines herself and Brett as the main characters. This good soul has been there. She knows the struggle. Her words are honest and carry more weight than the sessions that Gabby has with her psychologist.

Gabby's dismissal of the night nurse becomes almost routine. She was hopeful that in sleeping next to him, caressing his muscles and loving him, he would improve, but as the weeks drag on without any progress, it's a clear sign that her plan's failing.

With her confidence fading for Brett's improvement, her emotional state teeters. She fails to concentrate when reading, has emotional outbursts, and finds Brett's physical care exhausting.

When Mary, the day nurse, went on break, taking a stroll around the house, Gabby overheard her through an open window, mentioning during a phone call that Gabby was burned out, should leave her husband's care up to the hired help, and that she would benefit from a vacation.

Later that evening, her daddy asked her to go with him and Rita to Fort Worth to buy cattle and perhaps go on a shopping spree. Was this a coincidence, or was his suggestion a result of that phone call? Little things such as this caused her to be secretive, so when Brett started having more seizures, and the different medications weren't helping, she didn't record all of them. She fudged the numbers on the frequency and the duration.

Every day is a repeat of the day before. She hasn't played tennis or worked at the horse center. She has ceased texting friends and ignores incoming phone calls. What is she to say…no changes? She doesn't need to be reminded. Her stepbrother, Stan, and his girlfriend, Marie, who live down the lane, do a quick check-in every so often and sometimes hand her a casserole on their way to work at the horse center. That's the only contact she's had.

She's tried painting but ends up throwing one canvas after another into the trash. The colors don't mix right, and the brushes don't respond with the correct strokes. Her heart isn't in it. Worst of all, her insomnia has returned, and the caregiving, even with the help of nursing staff, is becoming overwhelming. As time ticks along, she's becoming more and more emotionally drained. The self-sacrifice is numbing.

Then, one afternoon when she was sure that all hope was gone and that her life without Brett would be meaningless, her doorbell rang, and with Liz's urging, she answered the door to Richard Wright, her former fiancé and the current US State Senator of Texas. It's that visit that set off her current state of depression and guilt. That evening she had believed Richard had thrown her a lifeline. Now, she deals with remorse and regret.

CHAPTER 5

July

Early in the morning, Richard knocks on the front door of Gabby's ranch house. Glancing out the small side window, she sees him brushing off his suit jacket and straightening his tie. He's one of the few men in Texas who still wears a suit and tie. Someone from the main house must have opened the gate and failed to warn her that he was coming to visit.

"Gabby, I know you're home. Open up. We need to talk." He runs his hand through his thick black hair.

She wishes he would go away.

"Come on, Gabby, please."

The banging is annoying and getting louder. Her brain prompts her to scream, "Stop it!" Instead, she places her hands over her ears.

"God damn it. I'll break your door down. Don't think I won't."

That man is so irritating. Throwing her hands up in the air, still in her bathrobe, her hair disheveled, she cautiously opens the door a crack while keeping the safety chain latched and her foot pressed against the bottom of the door.

His face is red. His hands are on his hips. "We need to talk. Let me in."

"No, go away." Her head drops, and she bites her lip as she narrows the space between the door and the frame, her foot strong on the base of the door, ready to close it.

"I had to drive all the way out here. You don't answer your cell. Why? It's been over a month. I don't have time for this." He looks up to the sky. "I'm in the middle of a campaign. This is the most important move in my career. How do you expect me to focus? It's not like this is going away. We need to deal with it. Come on, Gabby, help me here…meet me halfway, I'm trying." His once angry tone has changed to one of defeat. "You're so stubborn…always. For once, can you be an adult?" He rubs his forehead.

His words cut to her core. She's not a spoiled little girl. She's facing huge problems that no child or adult should have to face. But it's Richard, and from their past, she knows that staying calm is key, so she'll ignore his stinging remark.

"Sorry, I'm really sorry. Please go away. Brett needs me." She gently closes the door.

However, this small act refuels that previous dying amber, and he rages again.

"Gabby, Gabby, open up." He resumes hammering on the door, and she's surprised when the noise abruptly stops. Persistence is not one of his virtues; however, giving up so easily seems out of character, so much so that she's tempted to pull the sheer curtain aside for a peek.

"Gabby, listen to me. This is serious. If the press gets wind of this, there'll be hell to pay. We need a strategy. Gabby, please…" His voice trails off, and after a few seconds, he says, "Okay, remember this is on you. Don't say I didn't try."

She steals a glance, careful to stand to the side of the window. His mouth is still moving as he walks, and he rubs the dust from his black Bally shoes. She lets out a spontaneous chuckle watching him struggle, thinking, *Poor Richard. The perfectionist got his Bally shoes dirty. If a paparazzi's photo of the senator hit the tabloids, it would certainly ruin his respectable career, so he would think.*

He backs his red sports car out of her driveway, scattering stones and sending the dust flying as the car speeds down the lane. She bites her nails. He'll be back, and he's right about one thing—this will not go away.

She and Richard have a complicated history. It all started five years ago. After joining the city's most prestigious law firm and anxious to advance his career, the young, ambitious attorney eagerly added Wayne King to his client list. He was living his dream, and when his dealings with King led to meeting his beautiful daughter, the handsome couple's relationship was straight off the pages of a fairy tale. As he rode the waves of career success, the unfamiliar power led to arrogance, resulting in impulsive behaviors and poor judgment. When he started taking Gabby for granted and cheating on her, their happily ever after romance was ruined. Before Richard could show her how sorry he was, Brett quickly gained Gabby's attention, and she never went back to Richard, regardless of his efforts.

In addition to the unfortunate end of his relationship with Gabby, his relationship with King also became clear. Richard had been naïve to believe that he was the man in charge. However, King's big plan from the beginning was to groom Richard to take care of the ranchers since both the oil and cattle industries are heavily regulated. These powerful men, known in high circles as King's men, needed a politician in their back pocket to do their bidding. Richard is their pawn, and in many incidences, Richard feels the pressure. However, the perks and the power keep flaming his fiery ambitions, and the governor's mansion is the real estate that will be up for grabs the following year. He fancies the idea, regardless of its heavy price tag.

Gabby puts Richard out of her mind as best she can while brushing Brett's teeth and combing his hair. She likes him to look cared for when the nurse comes for the morning shift because that makes her feel as though she's a good wife. And after Richard's visit, she needs to feel good, or her guilt will certainly swallow her up. It seems her secret will soon be revealed to the world.

Today, after her unexpected visitor, she doesn't have time to shave Brett before the day-shift caretaker arrives, but that's okay. She likes the bit of scruff on his face. It's as if he's made the decision not to shave, which was his norm before the accident. She likes to pretend he's able to make those decisions. It's silly, but pretending and reminiscing is how she occupies her mind, how she tries to maintain her sanity during these long days.

He jerks once and then again. The ventilator bucks and chimes, alerting anyone within earshot that something is wrong.

"No, no, not again," she cries. She glances at the clock. The doctors want to know the duration of the seizures and whether they are generalized or localized to one side of the body. His whole body convulses.

"Please stop. God make it stop." She covers her eyes with her hands as if that will cease the seizure.

Minutes later and still seizing, his face turns dusky, his lips a blu-ish-gray hue. She grabs the Ambu bag. Disconnecting the ventilator from the tube in the opening of his trachea, she attaches the bag and forces precious air into his lungs. She has performed this act many times before, but that doesn't stop the adrenaline that surges through her veins.

"No, no. NO…" she pleads as beads of sweat form on her brow, reminding herself to stay the course even though her heart races. Her trembling hands compress the balloon-shaped object, and she counts out loud, "One…two…" deflating the bag to let the air escape before pushing more into his lungs.

What seems close to an eternity later, his face returns to a pale shade of pink. His body still spasms, but the movement wanes in intensity. *Thank God.* Unaware that she's been holding her breath, she breathes in deeply. She glances back at the clock, shaking her head in defeat. This seizure lasted well over thirty minutes. With the crisis over, she rests her head on his bed, allowing the linens to absorb her sorrow.

It's clear none of the medications are working. The initial brain scan showed damage, and the doctors explained that if the seizures occur more frequently and are longer in duration, more damage is inevitable. Little by little, her husband is slipping farther away.

From the sound of a car door closing, she knows the day nurse has arrived. Gabby's lied to them, the nurses and the doctors, by pur-posefully failing to give accurate accounts of Brett's condition on her watch. Quick to get rid of this seizure's evidence, she returns the re-suscitation bag to its rightful place. Like yesterday and the day before, she'll keep this a secret. She straightens his hair again and wipes the spittle from the side of his mouth.

Some days, like today, Gabby's grateful for the break the nursing staff provides. It's not even 9:00 a.m., and after Richard's visit and the seizure, it feels like the sun should be higher in the sky.

An hour later, a more composed and freshly showered Gabby drinks her second cup of coffee. Sweet memories come to mind as she holds the warm mug, a wedding present from her best friend, Ella. Ella had the pink mug etched in gold with Gabby's and Brett's wedding date. After taking a sip of the steaming brew, her finger wipes a lone drop from the rim. These past four months, she's missed the long chats with her sorority sister because Ella never fails to make her laugh. When was the last time she laughed? She can't remember.

Ella and Gabby have many shared memories. Being Ella's friend hasn't been without its difficulties, though. In college, Ella was a free spirit who did many things in excess. She drank too much, flirted too much, and was very impulsive. Many times, Gabby played the role of the mother figure, but then Ella's life changed.

More than a year ago, Ella married Gabby's stepbrother, Will, and just a few months ago, they welcomed little Gracie into their lives. Due to Brett's condition, she hasn't allowed herself to visit her best friend and meet her daughter. She wonders if she confided in Ella and voiced her sin, would her secret be safe?

In addition to missing Ella, she misses her work at the Equine-Assisted Therapy Center. She founded the organization and is thankful that the center is being run by Stan, her eldest stepbrother, and his partner, Marie, the horse therapist.

A dark cloak of sadness hovers when she thinks about how in the short duration since Brett's accident, both their lives have changed.

They are young and should be enjoying their first year of married life, planning their future. Instead, he's comatose, and she's stuck. She's navigating uncharted territory.

CHAPTER 6

As she closes the fantasy novel on her lap, Gabby would like nothing better than to get lost in an imaginary world, one filled with women who have superpowers and wear suits of titanium, who catch rides on the backs of beetles and dragonflies as they flit from one giant flowering treetop to another. However, lately, she can't seem to concentrate, and the words hold little meaning.

A noise from outside begs her attention. It gets louder as it gets closer. *Well, that's strange. Horses' hooves?* She places her book on the end table and peers out the front window. Her daddy is meandering up the driveway on Monster, and he's leading her horse, Lady. She makes a mental checklist, and no, she's certain they hadn't had plans. The only dates or appointments on her calendar are with medical staff.

He dismounts, ties the horses to her porch railing, and rings the bell. She may have been able to shoo Richard away, but her daddy, well, that's a different story. *Did Richard tell him? Gabby, don't panic.*

What a day this is turning out to be. Here goes, she thinks as she opens the door.

"Good morning, Princess." He tips his hat. "You've neglected your horse. Lady doesn't deserve that, and I didn't bring you up that way. You have responsibilities, so get your riding gear. We're going to go for a ride." There's a pause. "No excuses, the nurse is here." He nods toward the car in the drive and crosses his arms. Gabby knows this posture. It means serious business, and it's not just about her horse getting some exercise.

She shields her face from the sun. "I really can't."

He rubs his chin and places his hands on his hips. He stands firm. "I'm not asking."

"He told you?"

King nods. "Get your riding duds. I don't have all day."

"I'm going to kill him. Damn. How dare he?"

"There's a lot at stake. It's not just about you, my dear. I'll hear your side, what you want out of this, and then we'll make a plan. You got yourself into this, remember that, but moving forward, you'll play by my rules. Get movin,' Princess."

She turns and closes the door behind her, leaving him outside. He sits on the porch rocking chair, and she purposely doesn't offer him a cup from her pot of morning brew. It feels like time has turned back twenty years, and she's a child getting scolded. *What right does he have to treat me this way? He knows my situation.*

Inside, she gets dressed and dials Richard's cell. It immediately goes to voicemail. "I'll never speak to you ever again, you son of a bitch." She lets out a long sigh, then throws her phone on the bed. Her gut reaction is to avoid Richard's future calls, but the nurse can't reach her without her phone if something happens to Brett. Reluctantly, she picks it up and puts it back in her pocket.

She ponders what she'll tell her daddy as she dons her boots. This is the first time anyone has asked her what she wants since Brett's accident. In all of these long, painful months, not one person has considered her needs and desires. She certainly would not have picked this current situation to be the reason for this breakthrough. But here it is, and there is no getting around it.

Everyone has been focusing on Brett's condition and needs. Over these past few months, there have been endless decisions about his care, and she has made them all. Rarely does she ask family for advice; however, at times, the advice flows freely. Even perfect strangers have offered unsolicited advice, folks she's met in hospital waiting rooms, people who know nothing about her circumstances but feel obliged to offer their opinions, doing it all under the guise of being helpful. For this reason, she's put effort into distancing friends and family, attempting to hide her pain, her unhappiness, and her struggles. She doesn't want their pity. Pity isn't going to bring Brett back.

Welcome to her new life. Her former life was close to perfect, almost too perfect, and for that, the universe decided to rip it away. How will she answer her daddy's question? What does she want to do about this most recent crisis?

The truth is she needs someone to tell her that she's a terrible person, that she's an awful wife. Her daddy seems upset about this developing situation, although he won't hate her or judge her. She's done a good job of that already, punishing herself by pushing others away because she believes that if she stays secluded in her house and dutifully cares for her husband, she's making restitution for her sin.

She wonders what she was thinking that night in May. Was she weak and needy, or was she assertive and daring? For that one night, she took off her steel armor of pity and loneliness and allowed herself freedom. One night to escape her painful reality. And now that night haunts her and will change her life forever.

With boots on her feet, hat and leather gloves in hand, she checks the mirror and throws back her shoulders, holds her head high. She's going to confession. She's guilty of the crime, and it's time for the verdict.

Boldly, she opens the porch door, then steps out and turns. The sight before her is just the opposite of what she expected. Her strong, confident daddy rocks in the chair, and is it the sun, or is there a tear streak that has left a trail down his cheek? It takes her breath away.

"Ready?" She turns. How will she handle this? *He's the strong one—always in charge, always knowing the right thing to do.*

"Don't mind an old man. I'm missing your mama. Wish she were here. Days like today, sitting here on your porch. I miss her... my Anna, my sweet Anna."

"Aww, Daddy. I miss her too. I'm so sorry."

He stands, places his hat back on his head before unhitching her horse. "Need a lift?" He winks and offers his interlocked hands for her to use as a step.

"Of course not." She puts her boot into the stirrup and swings her leg up over Lady's back. "I'm still your daughter."

"That you are. I wouldn't have it any other way."

They share a smile, and she leans down to pat Lady. "I've missed you," she whispers into the mare's ear, then is reminded of her habit of bringing Lady a treat. This time, she's forgotten the apple. "Sorry, girl." She gives the mare another pat.

Her daddy mounts and turns to the path along the lake. She follows, tipping her head up to catch the sun's rays, the warmth giving her a hint of hope. The birds' calls are cheery, and the rustling of the leaves welcoming. She's forgotten more than the habit of apples for her mare. For weeks, she's been a prisoner in her house, keeping the drapes pulled, refusing invitations to meals at the main house, and making excuses for not allowing friends to visit. She's even quit answering calls from her best friend, her sister-in-law, Ella. "Sorry, it's not a good time. Brett's therapist is coming in a few minutes." Always promising to make a date soon but never following through.

"A beautiful day." Her daddy waits for her so they can ride side-by-side.

"This was a good idea. I forgot about Lady. Thank you. Guess I've been pretty terrible lately."

"Yep, you have. You're under a lot of pressure. We're all concerned and have tried to give you the space you requested."

"I...I..."

He doesn't let her finish. "Beautiful day," he says again. "Let's go." He spurs his horse into a canter across the meadow, then to a trot.

"Ok, you're on." She kicks Lady, and off they gallop. This is the same field where she showcased her riding abilities to Brett on his first day at the ranch. That was a fine day. It had been a different time of year, and there were wildflowers, the earth alive with the scents of spring. She and Brett were feeling vibrant as their love for each other was budding. However, that's not the case today in late summer. The leaves are tipped with yellow, and the grass is brittle and dry—a perfect parallel to her current situation.

The wind blows in her face, nudging her out of her thoughts and pumping blood through her arteries, giving new life to the deprived tissues. She's tried to pretend that she's been dead to the world in an effort to share her husband's fate. They are a couple. What one experiences, the other does as well because that's how it is when you love someone. *Happiness is not allowed because I need to share in your suffering.* However, riding in the wind under the sun jogs her body, mind, and soul with reminders that she is very much alive. A wave of guilt gushes in her gut.

Is it this dawning realization or her lack of conditioning from sitting around for four months that causes her to gasp for air?

"Guess I'm a bit out of shape."

"We can stop. Over there, in the shade of that oak." He doesn't wait for her, just signals Monster to trot off in that direction. Catching her breath, she guides Lady to follow.

King dismounts, ties Monster to the tree, then removes the saddlebag and a blanket roll.

"Perfect place for a snack, and there's cell phone coverage." He holds up his cell and checks the bars. He takes out some brisket sandwiches, a bag with some of Jamie's homemade potato chips, and two bottles of sweet tea, then hands her a small apple.

The gesture turns up the corner of her mouth and prompts a small glitter in her eye.

"Thank you." She places her cheek on Lady's and feeds her horse the treat.

Gabby's stomach has no solid food in it, and recently early mornings have left her feeling queasy, but the chips are enticing. Jamie knows they are one of her favorites. Is it a coincidence that her daddy has brought them for their snack? She holds one in her mouth, and it seems to melt away, leaving savory salt on her tongue.

"Wow, I love these," she says, popping a second chip into her mouth.

DonnaLee Overly

"Jamie made them for you. You should come around a bit more. I thought hiring the nursing staff would give you some time to get away, maybe time to stop by and visit your old man or ride your horse."

"It's really hard, Daddy. I hate leaving Brett." She looks up at the sunrays shining through the tree.

"I understand that since Brett's been having more seizures, the doctors want to check his brain activity. Run some tests."

"What's the use? The tests will be the same, and it hurts to move him. I don't want to put him through that. I'll be able to tell when he shows signs of improvements."

"The doctors think the tests will show significant changes. The nurses report that some of the seizures have lasted nearly an hour."

She casts her eyes downward. He's raining on her parade of hope.

"Gabby..." He rubs her shoulder. "It's a come-to-Jesus moment, Princess. It's painful, and I can relate because I know how I felt when your sweet mama passed with cancer."

She rubs her forehead, and her eyes flow with tears. "What? You're giving up on him?"

"The nurses tell me..."

"The nurses. What do they know? No one knows. We need to be patient. We need to give him time." She turns and looks out over the meadow, choking back the burning anger.

"Gabby, the medications aren't working. I've spoken to the doctors." He takes a swig of sweet tea. "I'm going to tell you a story. When we get a longhorn into the gate during branding, he's bucking and all upset 'cause he's trapped. He doesn't take to the confined space. When we open the gate, he gets out fast. He runs into the pasture, and seconds later, you would never know what he had gone through just

47

a short time before. That's how I see our Brett. He's hurting, confined in that body. Think about it, where is Brett happiest?" He pauses a few seconds. "He's happiest when he's out on the range, riding his horse. That bed is his confinement. We would be doing him right to open the gate to his freedom. I love him like a son, and I know in my heart that he wouldn't want to live this way."

She looks up with a wrinkled brow and sniffles. "You're asking me to let him go?" She pushes away. "I can't do that, Daddy."

He pulls her into his chest and strokes her hair. "I know how much you love him. I'm askin' you to let the doctors run the tests. Then we can make an informed decision. We should go through this together. You've been shouldering this burden alone…shutting us out. For months now, I've been getting reports from the staff: your daughter's not eating, your daughter sits and stares out the window, your daughter…"

She sits up straighter, a fire behind her eyes. "Stop it. What do you expect them to say, your daughter is singing and dancing?" She stands and screams, "Your daughter is grieving. Her life has been ruined. The love of her life doesn't speak, doesn't eat, and probably can't breathe on his own! I'm trying to cope, to accept it, but it's hard. It's so damn hard."

He hastens to hold her. "Hey, hey, I know, Princess. Please, let's do this together. It's our loss too. Accept our offers of help, come over for dinner. It's like we've lost both Brett and you. I miss my family, *our* family. I'm not asking you to stop hurting, I'm asking you to let us in, so we can do this together. Look at you, I see my beautiful Gabby, and it tears me apart. Surely you can see you're putting your belt in a different notch. Honey, you need to think about the baby."

The baby. Her eyes open wide. The silence is penetrating. She's going to be sick. *My God.*

"The nurse found the pregnancy test in the trash. Gabby, I pay the bills, and they report to me. That's how it works. I've waited to hear this from you. I've given you space, but now it's not just about you."

"You told Richard…"

"No, I didn't tell Richard. The nurse wrote it in her report at the agency, and then the transcriptionist…let's just say, she's looking for another job. But I think the gossip has stopped because nothing has been reported in our local papers. They only know that you're pregnant. They don't know who the father is."

"How long have you known?"

"A few weeks."

"…a few weeks?"

"I can't wait any longer. The election is a little more than a year away. The schedule is full. Richard needs to be on top of his game. I can't have him distracted. He could be our next governor. Everything we worked for, everything I've put into place for years, and now my candidate is running around crazy, and it's my daughter who's…"

"What? Say it… screwing everything up?"

He chuckles. "That's a good choice of words, considering the circumstances."

"Unbelievable." She throws her hands up in the air before quickly covering her mouth. She leans over behind the tree and vomits. *What a nightmare.*

When she straightens, her daddy is close behind, offering a napkin.

"I'm sorry. I'm sorry about Brett. I'm sorry about what you've been going through, Gabby. But I'm not sorry about the baby. I need you to know that. I'm guessin' from the way you've been actin' that you feel guilty, so you keep to yourself, dutifully staying by Brett's side day and night and avoiding Richard and us. I can understand your inner turmoil, but I also understand why you let your guard down. Richard can be quite charming. No one's here to judge. Honey, the day after Richard spent the night with you, he was flyin' as high as a kite. He's always loved you. Surely, you know that. He has hopes that your relationship will continue, but you've shut him out. Now, the baby does complicate matters. There is still a baby, right?"

"I haven't miscarried, and no, I haven't had an abortion. Surely your loyal employees would have squealed." She hangs her head, realizing the remark sounds coy. *Who is this disrespectful gal?* She could never have imagined speaking to her daddy with such harshness.

"I'm so sorry, Daddy. I never meant to make a mess of things."

He places his arm around her and squeezes. "Even messes can hold unforeseen blessings, remember that. Babies are always a blessing."

King's cell rings. "Uh-huh. Okay. ...pause...she's right here. Hold on." He turns to Gabby. "Brett's had a long seizure. The nurse wants to call an ambulance to take him to the hospital. I think that's the right thing to do. Tell her to send him." He hands her the phone. "Tell her yes."

She bites her lip, hangs up, and hands him his phone. "It's done." There's a defeatist tone in her voice. "It's not what I want."

"Thank you, Gabby. You may not want this, but that doesn't change the fact that it's the right thing. In time, you'll come to realize that." He folds the blanket. "Let's go meet them at the hospital."

He wraps his arms around her small frame once more. "You got family who'll help you. Everything will be all right. We'll continue this conversation later."

50

She lowers her eyes and shakes her head. Her heart and mind cannot be fooled. Her daddy, the man capable of fixing so many problems, cannot fix her Brett. A familiar verse from the nursery rhyme that she and her daddy used to read pops into her head… "All the king's horses and all the king's men couldn't put Humpty together again."

CHAPTER 7

King and Gabby return from their outing, arriving at Gabby's house before the ambulance. There isn't a hospital nearby in this rural area of Texas, and the drive from the ranch to the hospital is just short of two hours. If this were a dire emergency, a medevac helicopter would have been dispatched. The nurse stands as they enter the study that was transformed into a hospital room months ago.

"I'm sorry. He seems to have taken a turn for the worse. I gathered some of his supplies to make the trip." Then she places the circular band in Gabby's hand. "I thought it best to give you his ring. They'll remove it as soon as he gets there, and trust me when I say it's safer with you. "

Unprepared for this tiny gesture that carries a huge implication, Gabby turns pale, her knees wobble. Her daddy offers a steady arm, and the nurse is quick to offer a chair.

"Gabby…" She hears a faint voice, but the ringing in her ears muffles the tones.

What is happening?

King carries his unconscious daughter to the couch. The nurse returns with a glass of water. Gabby's skin is cold and clammy.

Thinking fast, the nurse pricks Gabby's finger, then runs the strip with the drop of blood in the glucose meter. It registers sixty. "She's hypoglycemic. She probably didn't eat breakfast."

King thinks back to their picnic and recalls that Gabby only ate a couple of chips, then immediately vomited.

The nurse says, "It's anyone's guess if she had any dinner last night. She's nothing but skin and bones. Go get some sugar."

The sugar dissolves quickly under Gabby's tongue, and she opens her eyes.

King moves her to a sitting position.

"You fainted. Drink this." He holds a glass of orange juice mixed with more sugar to her lips.

"I can't."

"You must. Can't isn't an option, Princess."

She takes a few sips and pushes the glass away.

"Try again. Drink it for Brett. He needs you, now more than ever."

King has always been a champ at motivating people; it's one of his most outstanding traits. She takes a few more sips.

"When did you last eat?"

She turns away.

"Gabby, you have to take care of yourself."

"Daddy, I don't need a lecture." She rubs her forehead.

The ambulance is in the drive with Rita's car following. Immediately, she rushes to King's side.

"What's going on?" She's out of breath and is wearing pink slippers.

King slips his arm around his wife. "Brett had another long seizure. And Gabby here fainted…hasn't been eating, and with the stress of it all… I'm worried." He searches the room. "Since they're here. I'll have them look at her too."

Rita rubs his arm. "You go and be with Brett. I'll sit with Gabby."

A short time later, Gabby remains on the couch with intravenous dextrose running into her arm.

"Another thirty minutes, and we'll be on our way with Mr. Matthews," says the paramedic. Then he signals over his shoulder toward Gabby. "She needs to eat. The injection I gave her should help with the nausea, and the dextrose will get her blood sugar up. Try to get something in her. If she can't keep it down, bring her in. The hospital isn't busy, so there are plenty of beds. They could even room together."

King nods. "I understand. Thanks for your help."

"Any time, Mr. King." He holds out his hand to shake before turning around. "Okay, boys, let's get him in the ambulance."

Gabby tries to stand as the stretcher wheels out of the room, but Rita holds her down.

"I need to go with him."

"Not this time. You heard the instructions. You need to eat, and then we'll leave for the hospital. The nurses and doctors will take it from here. They'll run tests first. If we go now, we'll just be waiting." Rita's hand on her back is warm, and she realizes how much she has missed human contact. The calming moment is brief; however, it is enough to remind her of the evening that started the mess she's currently facing.

Her eyes open wide, searching around her. "The ring, his ring, where is it?" Her high-pitched voice mimics the cry of a wounded animal. She jerks the cushions off the couch. "I've got to find it. "

In her panic, tunnel vision prevents her from seeing her daddy, who is standing close and holding the silver band with an outstretched hand.

"Gabby…Gabby," he says, each repeat a few decibels louder. "I have it right here. I put it in my pocket when you fainted."

As her eyes catch the perfect circle, relief washes over her face. She bends over with both hands on her thighs, panting as if she has just finished running a marathon. Exhaling and with a breathless tone, she says, "Thank God."

King removes the single gold braided chain from around his own neck, opens the clasp, and threads Brett's ring through before locking the clasp. Then he drapes the necklace over his daughter's head. He wishes that the rest of their crisis could be fixed as readily.

After eating scrambled eggs and toast prepared by Rita, King reaches for his daughter's hands. "I would give my life it that would fix things. I love you." He wipes his wet eyes. "So, tell me, close your eyes, and tell me your dreams."

Gabby laughs. "That's easy. I dream that Brett is whole again, and none of this ever happened. Can you be like Superman and reverse time?"

"That would be a solution. I am many things, but I'm not superman." He frowns as he earnestly studies her face. "Princess, Brett isn't going to get better. I'm sorry, but that's the reality. I can't change the past, and time doesn't stand still. We need a plan."

She pushes her chair back from the table. "I can't have this conversation. I need to get to the hospital." She stands and starts to clear the table. "Are you driving?"

"Of course. You're right. It's too much. Richard can wait. I'll handle him. Ok? He strokes her hair. "Come here," he says, pulling her in tight for a hug. "I love you, Princess. Even messes can hold blessings. Remember that. Together we can get through this."

CHAPTER 8

In the car riding to the hospital with her daddy and stepmother Rita, Gabby sits in the backseat and stares out the window. She doesn't see the passing landscape. Her body is numb. Her thoughts whirl like a tornado; she's so unsettled, she fears she'll go crazy.

A few weeks ago, she vowed not to subject Brett to more tests. She doesn't need scans to confirm that he's slipping further away. She slides his wedding band back and forth on the chain around her neck. As she reviews the morning's events, she questions if Brett really did have a second seizure or was this occurrence of events orchestrated to get Brett out of their home? The timing seems too perfect: Richard's visit followed by her daddy showing up with her horse, insisting they go riding, and the nurse's call shortly thereafter. *Why did the nurse call my daddy's cell? Shouldn't she have called mine?* Was her daddy using her situation as a smokescreen? Was he abusing her trust to manipulate? The anger flowing through her veins keeps her tears at bay. She'll fight back.

She's not willing to let go. She still has hope. Isn't that her job as his wife, think the best and wish for a miracle? It isn't fair. Their life together had just started. How does one prepare for this? It's unthinkable.

Today, Brett's tests will likely confirm that his condition has deteriorated. The long seizure activity is a good indicator of further brain damage. Besides that, he's ventilator dependent. What is she to do with this new knowledge…grant him permission to leave? The thought is terrifying.

The vision of the bull running free in the pasture from her daddy's story flashes in her mind. Yes, this is what Brett would want. It's painful to admit that her daddy is right. Brett would not want to live this way, but someone needs to explain how she will survive without him. In the past, there have been numerous times she contemplated dying with him. Now, it's not just her life that she would be ending. She ponders both sides of the debate of the beginning and the ending of life.

That debate brings light to another important question; what does she want out of life? She's always wanted to be a mother, and just one year ago, she lost a child. That loss sent her into a deep depression, but it was her art and love of music that pulled her through. Will this pregnancy push her through this challenging time?

Ironically, Richard was Jacob's father, and now she's carrying his child again. The timing for both pregnancies has been less than favorable. With the first pregnancy, she and Richard had broken up, and she had started dating Brett. Six weeks later, she was shocked to learn she was pregnant. Unable to explain that pregnancy, she escaped to the East Coast and nearly lost Brett. He came looking for her, confessed his love, and consented to raise her baby as his own. They never became a family because she miscarried in her seventh month, and little Jacob died.

Now, new life is once again in her womb. She prayed that Brett could be the father, but the timing makes that impossible. She closes her eyes and remembers.

It was about two months ago that Richard came to the house to pay a visit. He was checking up on her. He said he had promised her daddy. He brought flowers, little boxes of Chinese food, and her favorite wine. After the evening nurse's shift ended and Brett was tucked in for the night, Richard stayed. He was understanding and patient, listening to her every word. She felt like he cared; they laughed, and when she cried, he offered comfort and held her. And when her favorite song played, she begged him for a dance, and they floated around the room, their bodies merging a tiny bit more as the music played on, and slowly, they got reacquainted with each other.

When he lifted her chin and stole a kiss, it felt like they had traveled back five years to the time when they were a happy couple. He wedged open an invisible door, allowing rays of light into her dark reality, and drawn to the light, she followed it. She melted in the haven of his warm embrace and got lost in the scent of his aftershave. The tender human touch was intoxicating. When he made love to her, she imagined she was making love to Brett. She felt happy and whole. It was wonderful.

The morning after, Richard left before the break of dawn. He didn't wait for her to finish with Brett's care. He briefly paused, then waved as he walked out the door. His actions seemed to make light of their night together.

Later, her reflection in the mirror told a different story from what she had led herself to believe the night before. Staring back at her was an unfaithful wife who had cheated on her ill husband. Disgusted with her actions, she had vowed never to be so weak again.

To justify her reckless behavior, she told herself that Richard had taken advantage of her situation. However, even she couldn't convince herself of that lie. She had known exactly what was happening during those crucial moments leading up to him carrying her to bed, and she had willfully participated. She and Richard were familiar, and the familiarity felt casual, but this intimacy was dangerous. Aware that she still resided in his heart, she had played a selfish game. She needed to be loved and to escape the harshness of her reality. She hadn't cared in the least about the harm she would inflict.

In the days that followed, the truth of her sinful behavior was and still is hard to stomach. Her betrayal causes her to question her self-worth and is the reason she walls up inside her house and kneels at Brett's bedside, thinking that if she humbles herself and cares for his every need, every second of the day, her good deeds will erase that sinful night.

After making that decision, all of Richard's calls or texts went unanswered. She thinks that if she refuses to acknowledge them, he doesn't exist, and their night together was just a terrible mistake, a lapse in judgment. When she didn't get her period that month, she thought it had been delayed due to stress. However, with the daily relentless nausea, she ordered a pregnancy test online. She never thought that the staff would rummage through her trash, document their findings, and report to her daddy. They had exploited her trust. If they had done that, they were also capable of participating in the scheme to get Brett to the hospital.

All of this will have to wait. With time, someone will let their guard down, and the lie will be exposed. When this happens, she'll be ready. For now, her focus needs to be on Brett. She dreads going to the sterile, cold hospital. She doesn't wish to be confronted with the ultimate question. Her heart's heavy. Part of her wishes to take the easy route—to curl up, play the dutiful daughter, and allow her daddy to dictate Brett's future. The other side of her realizes that Brett needs her to be strong because she's his voice. She prays for sound judgment to make the right decisions. Can she put what's best for him above her own needs?

King swings the car into the circular drive at the hospital and unloads Rita and Gabby before parking in the adjacent lot. Gabby races into the lobby to the front desk to get Brett's room number and to have the doctor paged. She bites at her thumbnail, which is already down to the quick, and immediately puts her hand in her pocket so the receptionist cannot see how badly she needs a manicure.

"Mr. Matthew is in a private room, 2104. Sign here." She turns the clipboard to face Gabby. "Take the elevator to the second floor and turn left." The receptionist is an older volunteer. Her smile shows a missing front tooth where the tip of her tongue protrudes. She hands Gabby a visitor's slip.

"Did you page the doctor?" Gabby leans closer to the desk and reads her name badge, Rosalie.

"I'll send a text. We don't page doctors unless it's an emergency." She types on her keyboard and then takes back her clipboard. "Are you a relative?"

"His wife."

"I'll add that to the text, Mrs. Matthews."

King and Rita approach the desk behind her.

"We're together," Gabby says, ushering the small group toward the elevator.

The receptionist stands. "I'm sorry, only two people are allowed in a room at one time."

King falls behind, but returns before the elevator arrives.

"Have a good day, Mr. King. Nice to have met you." Rosalie is all smiles as she waves.

Rita hooks her arm into King's and looks into his eyes. "Using that old charm."

"Introduced myself, then gently informed her that my foundation built the hospital's west wing. That's all." He chuckles.

When they arrive at the room, it's empty, so King goes to the nurses' station. Gabby parts the sheer curtain and looks past the parking lot to the freeway, thinking that a freeway's a strange name for an Interstate Road. King returns a few minutes later with Dr. Bureau.

"Gabby…"

She jumps at the sound of her name, bringing her drifting mind back to the present.

"Sorry, what did you say?"

King repeats, "This is Dr. Bureau, the neurologist."

"Hello." Gabby turns but does not reach out her hand in welcome. Instead, she bites her lip and returns to looking out the window again. She takes a long, slow inhale and closes her eyes, attempting to brace for the doctor's assessment of Brett.

"It's a nice sunny day," she quips to delay the inevitable further.

King takes the lead. "Tell us about Brett's condition."

Dr. Bureau looks from King back to Gabby. "I have yet to see all the results because we are still running the last of the battery of tests. From what I have seen thus far, there have been some significant changes compared to previous records. I'll wait and give you the results when I have reviewed them thoroughly so I can answer all of your questions. Then together, we can make a comprehensive, informative plan on how to proceed. I'm glad that you brought him in. He's overdue; usually, we run tests monthly."

"We're glad he's here as well. We're also glad for your expertise, and we're thankful for Dr. James' recommendation. Thank you for taking Brett's case. I…umm…we feel a second opinion is warranted. We only want the best for him. Gabby, do you have any questions or concerns for Dr. Bureau? Gabby?"

"No, I have nothing. Like the doctor said, she doesn't have all of the results, so it's pointless to have an in-depth discussion." She faces the doctor. "Thank you. I appreciate you and everything your staff is doing." She offers a slight smile, which seems to break the tension that has been building in the room.

The doctor relaxes her shoulders. "We'll continue this discussion later." She leaves, and King follows her into the hallway.

Rita joins Gabby at the window. "I know it's tough when you love someone. Can I get you anything? Maybe we can find the coffee shop and wait there until Brett is finished with his tests. What do you say?"

Gabby pinches her lip. "Did you know about this?"

"About what, dear?"

"About having Brett brought here today. Did Daddy plan this?"

Rita rubs Gabby's back. "I'm not sure I understand. You agreed this was for the best."

A tear rolls down Gabby's cheek. "It doesn't matter."

"I'm sorry, honey. I'm really sorry. Let's go find that coffee shop." She pulls on Gabby's arm. "Maybe we can find some cookies, too. You know how your daddy loves chocolate chip cookies. Chocolate seems to make things better."

CHAPTER 9

Rita and Gabby head for the elevator. Before becoming her stepmother, Rita had been her boss at the art gallery in town. Gabby displayed her art and worked several shifts a week until she founded the equine center. The two women became fast friends, and it was Gabby who had introduced her daddy to Rita.

Rita tries to fill the hole that Gabby's mother's death left in the family. Their relationship has always been special. However, two months ago, Gabby stopped sharing. Rita's calls went unanswered and were sent to voicemail. The lack of communication was tough, but Rita respected her troubled stepdaughter's wishes. Now, the silence continues as they stand side by side in the closed space. When the elevator lowers to the main floor, the door opens, and they come face to face with Richard.

"I got here as soon as I could." He steps toward Gabby, reaching for an embrace.

Immediately, she raises her hand as if she's a cop stopping traffic.

"I can't deal with you. I won't deal with you," she says, pushing past him. "Rita, are you coming?"

Rita looks at him as if to say, *I'm sorry.* "Wayne is upstairs at the nurses' desk. He'll fill you in."

The elevator door closes.

"Who called him?" Gabby's brow is furrowed, and she bites her cheek.

"No one called him. He was at our house. You refused to see him, and he had driven all the way..."

"It's just like you to take his side."

"I'm not taking sides. I answered your question. You can't keep shutting us out...all of us, your daddy hurts for you, me and yes, Richard."

"I don't need a lecture."

"What do you need, Gabby? None of us can say or do the right thing. We're trying; we're all trying. I understand that you're under a blanket of stress, but treating the people who love you with such disrespect isn't helping us, and least of all you."

She pulls Gabby over to the side of the hallway, allowing an older man using a cane to pass. He tips his hat, and Rita cordially smiles in his direction before continuing the conversation with a lowered, firm voice.

"Of course Richard cares. He's not the bad guy here, and I feel sorry for him. There, I admit it, maybe you're right, and I'm taking his side." Rita looks squarely at her as if trying to see behind Gabby's eyes. "It's obvious he cares, and you treat him horribly. But apparently, you must have felt differently recently. For God's sake, you're carrying his child."

Gabby goes pale, and her mouth opens. However, no voice emerges. Rita's words sting; she feels as though she's been slapped. Nonetheless, they confirm her own belief that she's a terrible person. Her eyes well up with tears, and she starts to tremble.

"Oh, Rita, I'm so sorry," she sobs. "I'm a horrible person, a terrible wife...I want to die."

It is shocking to hear the words that suggest Gabby has traveled far down another dark tunnel. Depression had already wrapped its arms around her when she miscarried.

Rita hugs Gabby and is taken aback by the bony protrusions hidden by her blouse. "No one wants you to die. We love you, Gabby. No one is perfect, and we all make mistakes. You're not a terrible person. You are someone handling a difficult situation. Dealing with Brett by yourself all of these months seems to have taken its toll. It would be for anyone. And I won't even try to understand what's going on between you and Richard. But one thing I do know is that he's confused and upset that you refuse to speak with him. The poor boy is nearly out of his mind with worry. We all are."

"It's complicated...really complicated," she blubbers.

"Sometimes, we need help finding a solution. Seeking help's not a weakness; it is wisdom. Every problem has a solution. Please, accept our help." Rita pulls a Kleenex from her purse and hands it to Gabby. "I'm the one who needs to say I'm sorry. I'm sorry that your daddy and I weren't the ones to bang on your door months ago...before the situation got this far. Forgive us. Can you do that?"

She nods as she wipes her eyes but needs time to process Rita's apology. The sincerity she offers feels warm and earnest, the opposite of her previous cutting tone. Gabby's shoulders begin to relax.

"Let's go find that coffee. They have a beautiful courtyard that is taken care of by volunteers from the local garden club. It's supposed to be magnificent even for this time of year. We can have our coffee there." She leans on Rita as they continue down the hallway.

Gabby shields her eyes to block out the bright light in the court-yard with the sun shining on her face. The voice that has addressed her wasn't Rita's, however familiar, though she doesn't immediately put a face to it.

"Gabby, it's Carole, your psychologist. I apologize for startling you. I saw your father. He told me about Brett. I'm really sorry. My office should have insisted that you reschedule after you canceled your last appointment. Can we talk?" She looks at her watch. "I have a few minutes before I need to get back to the office. Tell me, how are you handling all of this?"

"I'm sure you know… it's the reason you're here. You didn't just bump into Daddy. He called you. I thought our relationship was supposed to be built on honesty. So, let's be honest."

"True, he called me. Your family is concerned, and rightly so. We agreed that if you started feeling out of control, you would call me. We've been together for over a year. I wish you would have reached out."

"I didn't."

"Can you explain to me why?"

Gabby bites her lip and looks over the trees. "It's complicated."

"Most crises are. Tell me about Brett." The psychologist puts her hand over hers.

"What's there to say? He did something stupid, and he ruined his life."

"You sound angry."

"He ruined his life. He ruined *our* lives."

"You feel like your life is ruined as well."

Gabby nods. "We had it all. We were so happy. Life was good… too good, so the universe ripped it away. It's not fair."

"Many things happen in life that we have no control over. We constantly need to adapt to change. How do you see Brett's situation changing? I understand that he is here for tests to reevaluate the extent of his brain damage."

"It wasn't my choice…these tests. My daddy and the nurses made this decision, not me."

"You feel you've lost control of your husband's care. Are you angry about how he got here, or are you afraid of the test results?"

Gabby doesn't answer, and a tear rolls off of her chin.

"It's hard to witness someone you love suffering. I admire you for being Brett's primary caregiver. It's a huge physical and emotional responsibility, but you can't give him the best care while neglecting yourself. That's a recipe for disaster. Call the office; I'll fit you in whenever. I want to see you tomorrow." Carole stands. "Until tomorrow, okay? One more thing, stay with family tonight. You shouldn't be alone." She turns back after taking a few steps. "Gabby, for what it's worth, I'm really sorry."

CHAPTER 10

Gabby returns to the coffee shop. Her daddy and Rita are sharing a table with Richard. When she approaches, they stop talking. Is she paranoid to think they are talking about her, or are they discussing Brett's tests?

"What's going on?" She searches each face for a clue.

Richard stands and pulls out a chair. "Here, have a seat."

"No, I'm going to check on Brett." She backs away from the group.

Richard approaches. "Gabby, please."

"Richard," King says sternly. "Brett's back in his room. Let her go."

As she steps into Brett's hospital room, the hum of the ventilator is familiar compared to the lack of contrast between her husband's pale skin and the white sheets. In this setting, he seems like a stranger.

73

Her head begins to whirl. On closer inspection, she sees that his hair is stiff, matted with gel where the leads were attached to measure his brain waves. In some spots, his head is shaved. What have they done? This is exactly the reason she didn't want these tests.

"Oh, sweetheart, I'm so sorry." She's going to be sick. She steps back and wretches.

"Mrs. Matthews, are you all right? She didn't hear Dr. Bureau's light steps.

"Sorry, I'm fine. How's my husband?"

"We've completed the tests. Compared to the ones taken a few months ago, there's been significant damage. Tomorrow, I'll run a breathing trial. We will take him off the vent but continue to provide adequate oxygen support. The test results will determine if his body responds to the rising carbon dioxide levels enough to trigger a spontaneous breath."

"And if he doesn't?"

"We'll return him to ventilator assistance."

"And what outcome do you anticipate?"

"Ms. Matthews, the test results already show your husband has suffered considerable damage. It's very unlikely that he'll recover, let alone breathe. The results of this test will give us vital information in deciding the next steps. Another prolonged seizure may be his last. As difficult as this situation seems, I'd like you to consider a DNR order and think about organ donation."

"What... a DNR?"

"Since he's already on a ventilator, the Do Not Resuscitate order will halt shocking his heart if it stops or prevent the administration of additional drugs."

"Let him die?" She reaches for his wedding ring that hangs from her neck.

"More like letting nature take its course. But yes, he would die."

She wrings her hands. "I'm not convinced we are doing everything available for this type of injury. Aren't there new experimental medicines… something, anything?"

"Ms. Matthews, if there were something, it would have been used by now. I'm doing the breathing trial for your benefit. In these critical times, having firm data is very convincing for family members. We've exhausted every option. I'm sorry. I'll ask the nurse to prepare the forms for your review. If you have any questions, have them text me." The doctor lingers, waiting to answer further questions. Finding none, she bows her head as if offering condolence and exits.

"No, I don't accept this. They're missing something." She rushes to the bedside and grabs his hand. "You're a fighter. You're strong. I need you. Open your eyes. Give me a sign."

Moments later, as she rests her head on his forearm, the nurse places the forms on the bedside table.

After her daddy and Rita return from the coffee shop, she doesn't acknowledge them. The private room's atmosphere is thick with sadness. Rita sits at the foot of the bed. Gabby hears her sniffles but keeps her forehead on Brett's arm.

After staring out the window and a failed attempt at small talk, King pulls a chair up next to his daughter. The action signals a familiar gesture, and as she had done as a child, she instinctively rests her body against his large chest. He strokes her hair just like he did back then.

75

However, unlike those previous intimate father-daughter moments, he can't reassure her that he can fix this and make everything better. He remembers the nights long ago, reading to her at bedtime, and how he always changed the last line of the popular children's rhyme. She'd giggle as he recited it...*All the king's horses and all the king's men put Humpty together again.* Many a night, they debated that line, and now, his greatest desire is to bring his version true. In this case, the original rhymester was right... *All the king's horses and all the king's men couldn't put Humpty together again.*

The reality of Brett's situation is written in stone. King rocks his daughter in his arms, and his tears fall on her face like a blanket of love, more precious than any words he may have uttered. The anger she felt about his manipulation to get Brett into the hospital has been long forgotten. As he gives in to his sorrow, she feels that they're one, grieving together for the first time in many months.

The tug on her heartstrings untangles the knot. She's been constructing a wall—first building it with bricks of hope and now demolishing it with a chisel cast from disappointment and guilt. As the callouses on Brett's hands have slowly melted away, her heart has taken them on, hardening as hope disintegrates. As she rocks in the warmth of her daddy's arms, her heart softens, and the wall crumbles. Humpty lies broken.

CHAPTER 11

Richard

In the small hospital chapel, a US State Senator of Texas sits in the pew and looks at the cross above the altar. Patience is not Richard's virtue, and he prays for the wisdom to say and do the right things. His behavior is critical for his future and the future of his heir. He prays for forgiveness, asking God to assist Gabby in understanding that they should be together. Not just for their child, but also for him, because during these past two years without her, he's been lost.

Their relationship, in Gabby's words, "is complicated." Complex but evolving, nevertheless, is his definition. In the past, he's made mistakes, but he's learned from them. Isn't that the whole point in life, learning from one's mistakes? When they were a couple years before, his ambitions and desire for success made him arrogant and proud. He did a bunch of stupid things—he drank irresponsibly and had reckless sex. His ability to get a quick hookup inflated his ego. The who or where didn't matter; it was about the adrenaline rush. Yes, he had been pretty brazen.

Is it a sin that his job, as well as his looks, score high? Women love the idea of being seen with a lawyer, especially one who captures the limelight as a politician. Combine that with his olive complexion, which accentuates his dark hair and eyes, as well as his toned body from daily workouts. He's been told he's a young version of George Clooney. Why does Gabby have such a firm hold on him?

Yes, his previous years had been full of mistakes. King had had to use his influence to get him out of jail when he got into a barroom brawl. All charges were dropped, and it was kept from the media. King has covered his ass repeatedly, and now that he's running for governor, his foolish days are over. He must walk a straight line, and who better to walk that line beside him than King's own daughter? Because she is still married, her pregnancy complicates their story. However, he will fight for the right to be a father. She can't be free of him, and for this, he's thankful. Currently, she refuses to speak with him, but she'll have to come around in due time. His hopes are high that they can start over again—God willing.

Brett's accident was unfortunate. Richard's not vindictive and would never wish anything bad on anyone, although he is one to take advantage of an opportunity, and that's what he did. He couldn't change Gabby's situation, so he used his charm to manipulate her. The evening he had planned went better than he could have ever imagined.

He couldn't have written a better script. Last fall, at Gabby and Brett's wedding, he thought he had lost her for good. Meanwhile, he tried dating other women. Amanda was a good prospect for a wife because she was well-posed, and the camera loved her. However, she came across as bossy. He doesn't appreciate a woman running his show, and his ego was bruised when it became clear that she mostly just loved his profession. He doubts that she truly loved him. It's been a cruel but worthwhile lesson, which causes him to reflect and take inventory of his previous relationship with Gabby.

When he and Gabby were a couple, had their roles been similar? Had he placed all the importance on the excitement and the power his profession offered, making her second best? He loved having Gabby on his arm, but he hadn't cherished her. He had been selfish, unfaithful, and a total jerk at times. Today, if he had the chance to do it all again, their relationship would be different. He's learned a lot over the years. He's changed. With the pregnancy, he feels that God's giving him a redo. For that, he's grateful.

No longer engaged in prayer, he closes his eyes, remembering their night together. It's etched into his mind and distracts him from the important duties of his job. The greater the distance she puts between them, the more he clings to his memories. It's making him crazy.

He reminisces about one afternoon, in particular, two months before:

That day he left the office early since things were pretty quiet. Earlier, King had called him about an oil bill that was in committee and then expressed his frustration over Gabby's refusal to have dinner with him and his wife. Richard couldn't stop thinking about Gabby. And he hadn't seen her since Brett's accident. He owed her a visit.

It was a calm, warm evening, so he picked up her favorite Chinese food and wine, put the top down on his convertible, and drove out to the ranch. One of the wranglers was leaving and waved him through the gate. When he arrived, Gabby stood on the threshold, flashing him a smile as he held up the bags with the square white boxes. They dined on the patio and watched the sun set. Their initial conversation included an update on

Brett's condition, and then they turned the discussion to their prior relationship. They laughed at his faults and of her little idiosyncrasies.

Shortly after the sun had set, the nurse motioned for Gabby. She reported Brett's vitals and handed Gabby the monitor that would alert if Brett needed tending. Richard kept her wine glass full.

After the nurse left, Gabby seemed to let down her guard, or maybe it was the wine that caused her to giggle at his dating stories. She swayed with the beat of the music playing overhead and extended her hand, asking him to dance. The scent of her hair was familiar, and it was as though he had come home. It felt so right, and the more they danced, the more her body seemed to melt into the curves of his body.

And then she cried, and he held her. He whispered kind words, telling her that he understood. When her knees buckled, he lifted her up. She wrapped her arms around his neck, and when he placed her on the bed, he kissed her. At first, she pulled away, but when he turned her to face him, she closed her eyes, and he uttered words of love, kissing her with a passion that scared him. He handled her with care as if she were made of porcelain, gently removing one piece of clothing at a time. She didn't protest. He undressed and laid beside her and then allowed his hands to do the talking. He made love to her, and it felt right.

In the morning, when he woke, she was gone from the bed. He dressed and stood in the hall, watching her care for her husband from afar. He couldn't force himself to go into the room. Not because he regretted his actions from the previous night, but because it was just the opposite. He had initiated his plan, thinking that it would take months to woo her. As he reflected on the evening, he realized it had happened so easily that perhaps she was the one who had used him. However, the young, naive woman he knew would have never done that. Could she have changed? Regardless, he needed to assure her that their night together hadn't been a mistake.

He wished to tell her goodbye that morning, but she was busy, and he had an early meeting. Instead of kissing her, he promised to call her later. He waved a quick goodbye before walking out the door.

He had tried calling her, had left at least a half a dozen messages that day. He had tried again the next day and the day after that. For weeks she refused to acknowledge him. He only got tidbits of how she was doing through her daddy. Wanting more, he started visiting the ArtSmart Gallery, hoping to find her there. He never did get that lucky, but if Rita was behind the counter, he could pump her for information.

Since Gabby has kept him at bay, the gallery is where he has felt her close. He would admire her work with more interest than he had had in the years they were together. Now, he regrets not supporting her artwork and for not encouraging her to pursue her talent. Staring at her paintings, he thinks that maybe if he had paid more attention, he'd have found clues to her mind's thinking pattern, giving him some knowledge that could help him in his quest to get her back. With each visit, his bond with Gabby's stepmother has deepened, and he's certain she is now an ally.

Upon reflection, if he could have a redo of the morning after he spent the night, he would have walked boldly into Brett's room and hugged her, looked her in the eyes, and told her he loved her. He would have done everything differently in hopes of a different outcome.

It was true that their relationship was complicated, and with the news that she is carrying his child, it is complex but continues to evolve. He has hope and faith, and of course, he has the greatest attribute of all, he has love. He bows in prayer again and fails to hear the chapel door open, followed by light footsteps.

CHAPTER 12

Gabby

Gabby sits holding her husband's hand. The familiar hum of the ventilator is gone, leaving only a thick silence. The white sheets that surround him remind her of a surrender flag. The battle is over. The medical equipment has been cleared from the room. Brett has been bathed, his hair combed. The nurses have been so sweet: offering their condolences and asking her if she needs anything. The chaplain came to pray with her family, anointed Brett, and left after marking the sign of the cross. Wanting time alone with Brett, she sent her daddy and Rita away. She wants to stay with him. She still needs him.

These past few hours have been a blur. However, has Brett made his own decision or was it the guided hand of God? Either way, the outcome is identical. Dr. Bureau had encouraged Gabby to sign the Do Not Resuscitate order. She refused, even though his brain reflexes were gone. By signing the DNR, she felt she was giving up on him, making her feel more guilty, so she continued to fight for his life. But his heart stopped, and even with the staff's interventions, it didn't restart. The doctors have pronounced him dead.

She strokes his face, then twirls his brown curls around her finger. She often performed this intimate act before the accident and continued it in these last months as his caretaker. When she closes her eyes, he's there. His emerald eyes shine, and his dimple is pronounced in the big grin his handsome face wears. They had made a beautiful couple, and they were happy. They played tennis, went horseback riding, and made love under the stars. Some would say the chemistry between them was undeniable. Their love was magical; he moved her like no other. She's not sure how to live without him.

She wonders if he is free. Is he riding his horse, galloping toward the light? Her face rests on his arm, and she strokes his chest. On her wrist dangles a braided red bracelet with a large gold knot. Kissing the knot, she closes her eyes and remembers the special blessing and the significance of it.

A few months into their marriage, she and Brett had taken a weekend trip to Sugarland for the Chinese New Year. Sitting on the sidewalk outside the Buddhist temple sat a monk wearing a saffron-dyed robe. For a donation, he would splash water from a brush to cleanse a person from past sins, then give them a blessing for the new year.

As he spritzed holy water on Gabby's face, her mascara ran black streaks down her cheeks. In what seemed to be an effort to rid her of the dark smears, the monk repeatedly splashed her. Brett had tried to show respect but broke into laughter because she looked like a drowned cat. To complete the ritual, the monk gave a blessing for good relationships and good fate by placing the True Lover's Knot bracelet on her wrist.

The bracelet had fulfilled its promise for a good relationship because theirs was close to flawless. Now, she struggles with the hand life has dealt them. If the bracelet stood for good fate, how could this have happened? She removes the bracelet with an angry jerk and throws the red circle on the stark white sheets. This should not be their destiny.

Standing in the hospital room doorway, Richard stares at the somber scene and hangs his head. His heart aches for the woman he loves crying at the bedside; death is never easy. After months of having regrets for not walking boldly into Brett's room after their night together to tell her that he loved her, today he wants no other regrets. However, instead of offering comfort to the grieving widow, he exits unnoticed. He'll be patient; she needs time.

King places his hand on Richard's shoulder. "It was inevitable. Deep down, she knows he wasn't going to get better."

"I want to do something, anything to help." He throws his hands up in the air.

King pats him on the back. "Your presence here is enough."

"I'm not sure she knows I'm here." He rubs his forehead.

"I'll remind her that you stopped by. Later, she'll appreciate that you were here. Y'all will have plenty of time to work things out after this has passed. Trust me."

CHAPTER 13

OBITUARY OF BRETT M. MATTHEWS

Brett M. Matthews died at Kingston General Hospital on July 11, following a prolonged injury. He was born April 8, 1987, near Fort Worth, Texas, to Mary and Jacob Matthews, both deceased. He loved to play tennis, ride horses, and ranch. He was on the rodeo tour, winning metals in tie-down events, and last year he earned a National Belt. He is survived by his wife, Gabriella (King) Matthews, and is preceded in death by a son, Jacob. A private funeral service is planned.

A few days later, standing at the family gravesite on the King Ranch, under a canopy of oak trees with the sun rays streaming through the branches, the minister's words take second to the sight of the young widow dressed in traditional black. His heart aches to comfort her, but she still keeps her distance. Her coldness toward him penetrates to his core. With the present circumstances, he respectfully avoids any contact between them. She would freak if she got wind of the rumor circulating among the press here at her husband's funeral. He bites his inner cheek; he must be understanding.

Earlier, the reporters had requested an interview:

Reporter 1: "Senator Wright, tell us about your relationship with the King family, why you've put the state's business on hold to attend Brett Matthews's funeral."

Richard: "Wayne King has been my client since I first moved here. I've become close friends with him and his family. I assure you the state of Texas is in good hands."

Reporter 2: "A few months ago, it was reported that drug lord Eugene Lopez was arrested right here on the King ranch. Can you tell us about your role in that sting operation?"

Richard: "Yes, a victim who had escaped was discovered on the eastern outskirts of the ranch. With my help, an operation to apprehend Lopez was organized, coordinated with several agencies—the local sheriff's department, the Drug Enforcement Agency, and the FBI. Working together, they apprehended and charged Mr. Lopez, as well as other top men responsible for running the human trafficking ring, one that extended beyond the Texas border into states as far away as Georgia and Florida. It was the breakthrough we needed to protect our citizens from this horrific crime and to get harmful drugs off our streets."

Pleased with the small band of reporters scribbling on their notepads and the cameras videotaping, he relished their attention with hopes for coverage on the evening news. He also prayed for a headline to grace tomorrow's front page. With the campaign for governor just a little over a year away, publicity in these early stages is crucial. His name needs to be familiar in every Texas household.

Reporter 3: "Senator Wright, is it correct that you were once engaged to the widow, Gabriella Matthews?"

Richard sucks in a breath before answering. *Why dig up the past?* Curious as to the man's employer, he searches for the usual press badge. There is none. "Yes, I was...a few years ago." He looks away and points to another reporter.

But Reporter 3 is persistent: "How would you describe your relationship today? Are you still close? You've visited the hospital daily."

Richard fakes a smile. *Is this a reporter or a private investigator? Maybe he works for one of those sleazy tabloids.*

Richard: "It was a time to offer my support. I'm a good friend of the entire King family, including Gabby...umm...Ms. Matthews."

Reporter 3: Surely, since you're in the family's inner circle, you're aware that Ms. Matthews is pregnant."

He tells himself to stay calm and carefully think about his reply, but his heart is racing, and perspiration forms on his brow. He bows out.

Richard: "Now, if you'll excuse me, I'm here for a funeral. Your respect is appreciated. Let's give the family the privacy they deserve. Thank you."

He turns.

Reporter 3: "But, Senator Wright, Senator Wright..."

He waves his arm in the air, and though he can hear footsteps on the gravel path behind him, he continues, careful to walk at a normal pace toward the cemetery, even though he wants to run. The footsteps get closer.

Many thoughts are swirling in his mind. He'd thought King had squelched the gossip. Chills run down his spine. He should have been prepared. What would King do? He reaches for his phone and clicks on the camera.

He turns, and with a steady voice, remains calm. "What's your name? I don't see your badge."

"Hunter, sir."

"Do you have a card?"

The reporter checks his pockets. "No, sorry."

Richard questions his sincerity, then politely says, "No disrespect, but I'm to be at the gravesite. Call my office for an appointment."

King will be pleased that he was so levelheaded. He didn't lose his cool. He was professional; he acquired a name and snapped a photo as the man searched his pockets for his card. Who is this man, and what are his intentions?

King's been a wise mentor over the years. One lesson he has learned is to back up a concern with tangible facts. Richard's certain that King will put his dogs on the chase.

Following the scripture and eulogy, it is time for the family and friends to pay their last respects. Unbeknownst to Gabby, behind her, walking in single file, are their ranch hands as well as some from neighboring ranches. As they approach, she recognizes a few men as fellow competitors from the rodeo circuit. One by one, they stop and nod to Gabby and King and then toss a coin on the casket, an older practice that signifies the coin thrower's presence and respect for the deceased. One cowboy pauses in front of her, just a second longer than the others, and she lifts her eyes in an effort to say, "thank you." No words are spoken, but the message is powerful. She had seen this ritual only once, as a small child when her uncle passed; however, that was many years ago, and it surprises her that the tradition continues. Now, these hard-working men are paying their respects to one of their own, and their thoughtfulness is deeply touching. Brett would be honored.

Slowly, the casket is lowered into the ground and covered with several shovels of dirt. Gabby, assisted to stand by Rita, drops a flower, and her entire body shakes under the weight of grief. The heart-wrenching scene causes wet eyes in the small group.

After the benediction is given, Richard, thinking many eyes are on him, shakes King's hand, nods to Rita, and gives Gabby a quick embrace. Even beneath her sunglasses, he senses the pain behind her mask. She's dealing with such an incredible loss.

This reminds him of the reporter's comments, which make him uneasy. She's better off not knowing. He doesn't wish for the reporters to hound her or possibly photograph them together in an attempt to create a sense of validity to whatever story they may manufacture. She deserves privacy. He'll make sure they honor that.

In the past, his dealings with the press haven't always been positive, so now that he is running for a prestigious office, he's careful to present his best self to his fellow Texans. It is important that they believe he is their best choice for governor.

The neighbors from a nearby ranch are the last to leave as the sun dips below the horizon. Gabby sits in a rocking chair on the porch with a glass of wine. Finally, a chance for Richard to get her alone. He pulls over a chair.

She raises her eyes and chuckles. "I'm not good company."

"I don't expect you to be. You don't have to say anything. It's been a really hard day."

"You have no idea."

"You're right, I don't, but that doesn't mean I can't sense your pain." He leans forward, and she drops her eyes. "I care about you." He moves to hold her hand, then pulls back.

"I should say thank you." Her tone is cold.

"I deserve the sarcasm. I haven't always treated you right."

"With sincerity, thank you for the apology. You didn't treat me right. We can agree on that." She takes a sip of her wine.

"The service was nice. Good day—sunny, clear skies."

"It's never a good day for a funeral." With firm conviction, she sets her wine glass on the table. "Excuse me. I can't do this."

As she stands, she trips over the rocking chair's runner, but his quick reflexes catch her. "Hey there. You okay? Take your time."

She's in his arms.

"I'm a bit dizzy."

"I've got you. Did you eat anything today?"

She bites her lip. "I can't remember. I drank wine today. I'm not supposed to, but to hell with the rules." She then announces sarcastically, "No wife can stomach her husband's casket being lowered into the ground." Her voice breaks, and she sobs.

He holds her tighter, and under his hand, her hair is silky. "I'm sorry, really sorry. It sucks. Please, let me help." God, he's missed her scent. He breathes deeply to get it inside his lungs. He wants a reminder to keep her close long after she's out of his arms.

Overhead, a flash gets his attention. Searching in its direction, he sees four red lights. He's sure it's a drone because the red lights dim as they move toward the direction of the main road. In the evening light, he's able to see the faint outline of a vehicle, a white truck, perhaps, if he had to guess. *Damn reporters. They're violating air space laws.* He wishes to raise a lone finger. No, a candidate for governor must be respectful.

This is not the coverage he wants. Thankful that Gabby is unaware, he assists her through the threshold into the house as he glances over his shoulder one last time.

"Let's taste some of your good neighbors' hospitality. What do you say?" He doesn't wait for a reply. "I'll ask Jamie to make a fresh pot of coffee, decaffeinated, of course. We could all use some sleep tonight."

With red eyes, she peers at him. "It's getting late. Are you staying? Her stare is pitiful, as if she's looking for a touch of hope.

"Yes, I'll stay if you want."

She sighs and says, "Good," then leans her hand against his chest.

Is her answer just the wine talking? Now, he's confused but happy nonetheless; so, let the tabloids print whatever they want. Today was a rough day, and tonight, he just doesn't care. He'll remove his politician's hat and be a good friend of the King family during their time of mourning.

CHAPTER 14

After the King household turns off the lights, Richard loosens his belt and removes his shoes and socks. He could never sleep in socks; they make his feet feel like they're in a sauna. He adjusts the pillows on the couch in King's office, his bed for the night. Earlier this afternoon, worried about Gabby, he texted his secretary, asking her to cancel his appointments for the following day. When he arrived this morning, he hadn't envisioned spending the night, but ever since the incident on the porch, he feels the need to be close. If he drove to his downtown condo, he'd obsess about the happenings at the ranch, so he's content to stay.

The clock struck midnight a few hours ago, announcing that it's officially Friday. He'll plan to stay the entire weekend. Close to Gabby is where he wants to be. Unable to shut his eyes in sleep, he parts the curtain, checking the surrounding fields for any signs of lingering reporters. The open window allows the night breeze to hit his face, and the moon shines on the barn's roof and the fenceposts, offering a soothing glow, breaking up the dark shadows. All seems quiet on this July summer night.

At a distance, there is a light from the Adams's property. Stan Adams, Gabby's stepbrother, came to the ranch last year to convalesce after fracturing his arm and leg in a motorcycle accident. During that three-month visit, Texas courted him, and he fell in love with her simple ways.

It was Rita's coaxing that persuaded King to gift some land to her son where his house currently stands. She reminded her husband of his wedding eve promise, how he had lifted his champagne glass and made a toast, declaring that her sons were now members of the family. King, a man of his word, and after seeing firsthand the joy and purpose the ranch life gave Stan, honored her request. Immediately, Stan sold his condo in Washington, D.C., and the foundation for the Adams residence was poured the following week. Stan, a quiet, middle-aged man, fled the guest room at the main house and took his Borador, Ryder, to live in the house before the work was completed.

Stan has a paid position at the Equine Assisted Therapy Center, the foundation that Gabby started. He schedules appointments, maintains the books, and orders supplies. He helps care for the horses and manages to sneak a ride in the saddle when business is slow. Recently, he developed a relationship with Marie, the equine-assisted mental health practitioner at the center, and has welcomed her into his home. Their relationship is the main reason she accepted the job, leaving her family in California.

Richard gained respect for Stan after they worked together along with the Feds to bring Eugene Lopez, head of a drug and human trafficking organization, into custody. With Stan's help, King was able to steer Lopez and his men into a canyon, where he was trapped and arrested. Marie was one of the victims, and Stan had probably saved her life.

However, Stan and Richard share a history, which created conflict long before the Lopez incident. Each had proposed marriage to Gabby, and both men had difficulty understanding how she chose Brett. But that's all in the past, and now Gabby's relationship with Brett is just that, in the past.

Delighted that Stan has moved on with Marie and encouraged by the outcome of his one night with Gabby, Richard is confident he can rekindle their relationship. He'll be supportive, give her time to grieve, and keep her close to prevent history from repeating. With her pregnancy, no one is going to get between them, and as she'll see, he's committed to the family they can be together.

CHAPTER 15

Good morning. Coffee?" King raises his eyes, acknowledging Richard strolling into the dining room.

"Sure." Richard runs his fingers through his thick dark hair, then reaches out to take the coffee from King. The smell of bacon frying is an indicator that Jamie is in the kitchen.

"Rough night? That couch isn't known for a good night's sleep. The very reason I don't go to bed if Rita is angry." He chuckles.

"I'm not complaining." Richard places his hand on his hip and leans to stretch his back before pulling out a chair. He rotates his finger around the rim of the coffee mug. "We may have trouble."

King senses the urgency in the younger man's voice. "Oh?"

"A reporter is aware of Gabby's situation, her pregnancy. He asked questions, trying to get confirmation."

"And…" King sits to face him.

"I evaded answering." He fumbles in his pants pocket for his cell phone. "His name's Hunter. I'll text you his photo. I didn't recognize his organization. Must be some small tabloid, or maybe he's a private investigator."

King raises his eyebrows. "I'll look into it."

"I asked for a card when I didn't see his badge. He didn't have one. There's something about him, almost like he's driven to snag the big one and make a name for himself." He shifts his weight in the chair. "And there's more…last night when Gabby and I were on the porch, a drone flew overhead."

"I'll be a son of a bitch." King stands, his brow furrows.

"Gabby had her back turned, and I ushered her into the house. I also saw an older model white truck parked out by the gate. I don't know if it belongs to that same guy." He shakes his head. "Those reporters are vultures."

King scratches his head. "For God's sake, a family member is dead. Decent folks would leave us alone. I'll get my guys on it, and good job, Richard. Thanks. Let's keep this between us."

Glad that King's pleased with his handling of the reporter, he leans back in his chair and savors the smells of breakfast, a reminder that he's a bachelor. His mornings never smell this good.

He searches the room. "Where's everyone?"

"Rita's in the shower. I haven't seen Gabby and don't expect to see her much before noon. Rusty is down at the barn, and Jamie's in the kitchen doing what she does best." He glances at his watch. "Stan and Marie are on their way to work. The first appointment starts at eight-thirty. That leaves you and me. Glad you're here. After breakfast, we'll hammer down the schedule for the next few months." He pauses for a swallow of coffee. "Got some people lined up for meetings next week and a few high-profile lunches with CEOs in the weeks to follow. These are critical for funding the campaign down the homestretch."

He hesitates, then gives Richard a head-to-toe inspection. "Plus, I scheduled another photoshoot next Wednesday—photos with a more casual look that will relate to the common folk. A western style instead of that suit you're always wearing."

Richard tries to smooth the wrinkles on his shirt. "I hadn't planned on spending the night."

King chuckles. "Rita will get you some proper garb. After breakfast, we'll go for a ride. If I remember correctly, your horsemanship skills lack a bit. When we campaign midstate and farther west, a man in the saddle will resonate with the people more than a city slicker."

Gabby lifts the covers over her head to block the sunlight streaming through the window. Daylight is a sign that she survived the night. Sitting up, she grabs her aching head. Then her stomach rolls. She's going to be sick. She deserves to be punished because yesterday, she put her pregnancy on hold. She needed something to dull the pain. The Valium she popped in the morning helped her get through the most dreadful day of her life. Then, as day turned into evening, the pain intensified. For relief, she allowed herself some wine. Rita had raised an eyebrow, then turned away. She escaped to the front porch to avoid further scrutiny after she refilled her glass a third time. When Richard pulled up a chair, he hadn't scolded her. She remembers that he was nice.

The well-deserved headache and nausea serve as a brutal reminder that life goes on. Her stomach reels again, forcing her out of bed.

There's a knock at the door. "Gabby, are you okay?" Rita opens the door a crack. "Sweetie, can I come in?" She doesn't wait for an answer.

"What time is it?" Gabby calls from the bathroom.

"Almost noon. I brought you some coffee. I put cream in it just the way you like it."

"Thanks."

Rita pulls the covers up and starts to make the bed. "It's a nice day. Richard and Wayne are out riding. They thought you might like to join. I told them to let you rest. Yesterday was a struggle." She fluffs the pillow. "Did you get any sleep?"

Gabby returns from the bathroom, sits on the bed, and lifts the mug to her lips. The coffee smells good and gives warmth to her cold insides.

"Bad day yesterday for all of us, especially you. People had the nicest things to say about Brett. He had a way of making friends wherever he went." Rita rubs her back. "How are you, really?"

"Not so good."

"I know it's hard. We'll get through this together, one day at a time. Come on down. Jamie saved you some breakfast. You'll feel better after you eat. Your baby will like that too."

"I can't." She reaches for her stomach.

"I'm not taking no for an answer. Come on." Rita pulls her up. "You've been strong for so long... alone, taking care of Brett. Now, it's our turn to take care of you. He would want that for you."

CHAPTER 16

A day later, Gabby visits Brett's gravesite. She feels a duty to check that his grave is undisturbed. It will also be her come-to-Jesus moment to lift the burden she carries. The mound of Texas dirt marks the spot since the headstone has yet to be ordered. She couldn't agree on the wording when the undertaker first showed her the brochure, but she doesn't feel the need to rush. A headstone isn't going to change anything. He's gone.

◇◇◇◇◇◇

Looking in from the cemetery gate, Richard sees her lower her head and senses her struggling against the pain. She asked him to give her time alone, so he's waiting outside the gated cemetery. He respects her wishes because he knows from his recent research on the grieving process that she needs to accept this to move forward. He paces back and forth, checking his emails and missed calls. It's Sunday, marking his fourth day at the ranch and his last. Tomorrow is a workday, and because he took an extra day off last week, his appointment book is filled.

In the family cemetery in the shade of large oak trees, the musty scent of the earth lingers in the air. After unlatching the iron gate, Gabby stops first at the grave of her infant son, Jacob. She kisses her fingers before tracing the letters on the marble that reads "beloved son." Then, cautiously approaching the newly dug grave, she removes her sneakers and socks, desperate for his energy, thinking it will flow up through her bare feet. She plucks a wilted flower from a wreath left on the fresh mound of dirt. The white rose still has a faint smell, and the petals feel soft against her cheek.

Tenderly pulling off one petal at a time, she then watches them flutter effortlessly to the place where he lies. As each one drops, she talks about the mundane—the weather, the ranch, and the birds flying overhead; however, these topics will not lighten her load. With only the last petal remaining, there's no more procrastinating. She sucks in her breath, then begins to speak what's on her heart.

She whispers, "God knows how much I love you. How am I supposed to live without seeing the twinkle in your green eyes before your dimple deepens, without your touch keeping me warm at night, without your love? I'm lost…so lost without you." She twirls the lone stem in her hand and looks up to the sky as if seeking God's forgiveness as well.

"I'm so sorry, Brett. I'm sorry for being weak. I'm a coward. I should have told you when you were still here. I tried to tell you…many times, but I couldn't bear the thought of you hating me."

The tears pour down her face, and she wipes them away with her hand. "Please don't hate me. I was lonely and messed up. I made a mistake. I know there's no good excuse." As she speaks, a cloud covers the sun. She kneels.

"I didn't know Richard was coming, not that it matters. I swear, I didn't plan it. But he came over with food and wine, and he listened, and we laughed, and it felt so good to be…normal again." She buries her face in her hands, sobbing so hard that the words nearly choke her. "I was unfaithful to you, and now I'm pregnant." She leans over and falls to the ground, whimpering. "Please, forgive me. I need you to forgive me."

Richard's pacing increases as time passes, and when she falls to the ground sobbing, he abandons her wish for privacy and rushes to her side.

"Come, it's time to go." He nudges her to get up.

She hides her face. "No, leave me be. I can't."

"Gabby, please get up. You've made your peace. It's time to go."

"Go away." She pushes him.

"I won't leave you…lying here on the ground."

When he concludes that with her stubbornness, the more he pleads, the more she'll resist, so he sits down on the ground. "If you won't get up, then I'll come down."

"I'm a horrible person."

He rubs her back. "You're not a horrible person. You're a hurting person. There's a big difference."

He sits with her, rubbing her back. His heart aches for the woman he loves. She lifts her head and rests on his knee. The touch of his hand stroking her blond hair gives her a sense of peace. Minutes pass, and the sounds of nature mix with their inner thoughts.

Her confession seems to have lessened her guilt. She observed that the earth didn't rumble, and Brett's grave didn't open. The birds continue with their song, and the light breeze hits her cheek. Brett's body, his prison these past four months, might lie under her feet, but she senses that his spirit and soul are elsewhere. She glances up to the clouds, searching for a sign of his whereabouts, for wherever he may be. She's not ready to say goodbye.

Lowering her eyes, she sees the dirt on Richard's pants and shoes. She laughs. "Richard, you've got dirt on you."

He tries to brush off the mud. "I never liked these shoes. They hurt my feet." He smiles.

She wipes her tears. "Richard, the man I once knew, would never have one speck of dirt on him."

"Maybe that Richard has changed."

She sits up and leans into him. He buries his nose in her hair. "Gabby, Brett would want you to be happy. Lord Tennyson put it this way… "it is better to have loved and lost than never to have loved at all.""

She looks up at him wide-eyed. "You're quoting poetry now?"

He smiles. "There's a lot about me that you don't know."

They continue to sit, and the sun moves farther across the sky to the west. Finally, he stands and pulls her up. "Let's go. Jamie will have dinner waiting for us."

She's reluctant to leave, and he doesn't wish to pressure her. "I'll give you a few minutes. I'll wait out there. Okay?"

She nods as he stands. "Thank you."

CHAPTER 17

August

King straightens the baby-blue tie that, according to Rita, brings out Richard's dark-brown eyes. "You ready? You memorized the answers in my email, right? You understand the magnitude of his support and the financial backing that comes with his company? This is important for us...for you."

Richard shuffles his feet. "I know...I know."

"How do I look? No egg on my face?" King wipes his face with his handkerchief.

Richard rolls his eyes. "What's wrong with you? I've never seen you this way."

King laughs and slaps him on the back. "That's a joke. Nothing's wrong with me. This is the brass ring, my boy."

"Okay, okay, this isn't my first meeting. I'll be fine."

Richard and King walk through the double glass doors of the historical Driscoll Hotel's restaurant, three blocks from the capitol building. Already seated is Steven Prime, founder and CEO of the biggest tech company in the nation. He moved his company headquarters to Texas a few years ago for the tax cuts and the incentives offered.

Richard takes the lead and extends his hand. "Mr. Prime, a pleasure."

"The pleasure's all mine, Senator. If King says that you're his man, then you're the candidate for me." He reaches back to shake King's hand. "Please, gentlemen, take a seat."

Prime gets right down to business. "Richard, tell me your angle and your priorities when you get elected. Notice I didn't say *if*." He laughs, which helps to put Richard at ease.

Their conversation takes off with fire. Richard and Prime are in deep discussion about the future of the tech business in Texas when Richard raises his eyes as he lifts his water glass. He sees a rather distraught-looking Gabby standing at the hostess podium.

Prime, clearly aware that he's lost his companion's focus, looks over his shoulder at the beautiful blond. "She would grab my attention as well."

"I'm sorry. Something must be wrong. Please excuse me." Richard jumps out of his chair. King stands, trying to grab his arm.

King is wide-eyed. "Steven, sorry. I'll take care of it."

Prime is amused. "No, please. Sit down. It's good for a politician to know his priorities. Clearly, this is an urgent matter. Let it play out. The woman is noticeably upset."

"The woman is my daughter." King bites the inside of his cheek.

"She undoubtedly takes after her mother." He winks at King. "You old goat. She's gorgeous. Is she hitched? The reason I ask ... look at them, it's obvious he cares. They make a handsome couple."

He turns back to King, and in a serious tone, says, "My greatest concern is that our man here is single. He'll get the young female votes, but that's a tiny percentage. Elections are won by courting the working class. They relate to someone like them, a family man. If he's single, everyone wealthy or poor, male or female, will question his judgment whenever a skirt with a nice pair of legs walks into the room." He takes a sip of bourbon. "When I got divorced, women came out of the woodwork. Even an old ugly bastard like me had more offers than I could manage. Those were the days." He chuckles. "But your boy has charisma. That can work for him and against him. Should I be concerned about Mr. Richard Wright? Many a politician gets caught. I would have placed bets on Gary Hart being in the White House, and we all know how that went."

King leans forward with both elbows on the table. "I understand what you're saying. Richard made some mistakes in his younger days, but he's matured and aware of the importance of the office. Unfortunately, you're right. Every political figure needs to be careful whether he's married or single. The press will print anything they believe will sell. Later, the disclaimer posted on an inside page will mean nothing. The public will only remember the scandal's headline plastered on the front page. Technology has its pros and cons. You're in the business."

"Touché, King. With access to social media, fake photos circulate. It's brutal." He leans back in his chair. "Getting him hitched will bring good publicity. Like I said, they make a handsome couple."

"My daughter is recently widowed. She's grieving and fragile. You saw the distress on her face. Richard has been very supportive through it all."

"There's plenty of good women in the Great Lone Star State. She should be classy and hot, but not too hot, have a clean record, an all-American gal. I'll get my guys on it. We'll leak information and photos, slanting them to our advantage. Since folks get tired of political ads flooding their television, this will be an incognito campaign. They'll be royalty, like Princess Di and Charles. It's a brilliant strategy."

King interrupts, "The crisis must be resolved. They're coming this way."

Richard steps to the side as Steven Prime stands. "I apologize for leaving the table so quickly. Please meet Gabriella King, um... Gabriella Matthews."

"Pleasure, Ms. Matthews, so sorry for your loss." Prime squeezes her hand and bows.

Gabby lowers her eyes. "Thank you. I'm sorry to have taken Richard away. I know your time is valuable. I'll be on my way."

"Nonsense. Join us." He pulls out the chair on his left side.

"I should go. I never meant to intrude."

"Please, I insist." Prime motions toward the chair. "Forgive me if I'm being too forward, but you seemed rather upset earlier. Is there anything I can do to help?"

"Really, it's nothing. It's embarrassing. I shouldn't let these things get to me." She senses his earnestness. "My husband's death certificate isn't filed yet with the county clerk's office. It seems the coroner hasn't submitted the paperwork. Until I have copies, I can't close accounts or transfer bills."

"Rob Stone can help. He's a friend." Steven places his hand over hers. " I'll make a call."

Within the minute, he places the call, gives the message, and hangs up. "See, easy. All done. Let's order lunch. Your document will be waiting when we finish." Gabby searches the blank faces of her daddy and Richard. Instead of looking at her, they stare at Steven. He's beaming, and his eyes are intently fixed on her.

Her face turns red, and she smiles, which makes his smile larger. "Thank you."

"Worth it to see a beautiful woman smile. Best thing I've done and seen so far today. Tell me about this guy here." He points to Richard. "Why should I back Senator Wright for governor?"

King did not send his scripted answers to Gabby. She wasn't supposed to be here. It's obvious that the man Richard needs to impress is engrossed with King's daughter.

Over the years, Gabby has heard many conversations between Richard and her daddy about politics and Richard's advancements up the ranks. She knows the stakes are high.

Since her high school days, she's been by her daddy's side as he has groomed politicians and courted wealthy businessmen. Her daddy has placed all of his cards on Richard's path to governor. Putting aside her grief and her problems, she'll need to step up and join in their efforts by giving Richard a glowing recommendation.

"I've known Richard since he came to town. He's won many high-profile cases. The numbers are…"

"Whoa there, darlin,' that's in the record books. I want and value your opinion." He leans forward, putting his arms on the table to get at eye level. "Forget he's sitting over there. Pretend it's just you and me having this little conversation, and you tell me everything you know."

Her face reddens again, and she rubs her forehead.

Prime laughs so hard that his belly jiggles. "Okay, well, not everything. You're going to have me blushing soon." He takes another sip of his bourbon. "Oh, to be young."

Her daddy looks as if he's swallowed a goldfish, and Richard's about to jump out of his seat. The future of the Texas government's highest seat now lies in her hands.

She pauses to put her words in order and clears her throat. "Recently, as I've dealt with my husband's illness and death, Richard has been a great pillar of support. He's been careful and protective of my privacy." She covers Prime's hand with her own. She knows the power of feminine charm. "Surely, you saw that today. I came here to speak with Daddy, and I no sooner walk into the restaurant when Richard offers assistance. I assure you that he'll respect our precious state and take great care of its citizens.

His experience with stopping drug distribution and his work capturing Eugene Lopez's human trafficking ring is just the beginning of the good work he's doing as a senator. Imagine the great things he will be able to do as our next governor." She squeezes his hand and closes her eyes as if savoring her next words, aware that she has lured Prime into her web. "Richard is thoughtful and conscientious and tough when he needs to be. No one can come close to being the decent man that he is."

King sits up straighter.

Prime searches each face, and it seems that everyone is holding his breath. "Well, that settles it."

Sighs of relief are heard around the table, followed by nervous laughter. Gabby reads pride in her daddy's eyes.

Prime picks up the menu. "Let's see what's for lunch. I hear they have great steaks."

As Prime focuses on his order, she lifts her water glass and smiles at her daddy and Richard as if to say, *I did good. Why were you so worried?*

"That sounds great," she says with a spark of joy that has been missing for the past few months. "I haven't had a decent steak in a long time. Thanks for asking me to join."

Prime shakes his head. "Pleasures all mine, sweetheart. Let's get you that steak." He turns in his chair. "Hey, waiter. We're ready to order."

CHAPTER 18

August

Ella, Gabby's best friend, holds Gabby's hand as the obstetrician moves the wand around her belly, spreading the conductive gel in a large circle. The quick *lub-dub* of the fetal heartbeat is the music they were set on hearing. Ella squeezes her hand tighter as the heartbeat becomes louder.

"This is so exciting," Ella squeals.

"Seems like it's more so for you," Gabby says.

"Really, Gabby, this is a new life. It's your baby. I never thought motherhood would be so grand."

"I don't want to get my hopes up, okay?"

"You need to put that in the past. This time will be different. You'll see."

Gabby strains her neck to look at the screen. "I hope you're right."

"Little Gracie is such a joy. I'm excited for you to get to know her. I rest better knowing that you're going to be her godmother. God forbid anything should happen to Will and me."

This is Gabby's first appointment, so the doctor is performing a full exam. She's hoping that by starting prenatal visits, Rita's harassment will stop. She understands that Rita means well, but her daily nagging is annoying. She's been vocal about her motives, saying such things as, "Once you hear the heartbeat, you will be more accepting of the pregnancy," and, "Perhaps thinking about the future with your baby will push your grief away."

With Ella visiting now, the two of them have teamed up under the umbrella of helping to make Gabby's life easier. Instead, they are making her life miserable. Ella and Will are visiting from Washington, D.C. with their six-month-old daughter, Gracie, who is presently at the ranch in her grandmother's care.

"There's your baby." The doctor turns the screen toward Gabby. "That little peanut shape. See those little buds? Those are the legs, and here are the arms."

Gabby bites her lip. With Brett gone, she thought her guilt would wane and she would become comfortable with her pregnancy. However, in keeping the rightful father a secret, she's still stuck. Not even her appointments with Carole, her psychologist, have made this easier.

"This is so awesome. With this baby, you will always have a part of Brett," Ella boasts.

A tear streaks down Gabby's face. She closes her eyes.

"I shouldn't have said his name. Is that why you're upset?" Ella takes her hand. "I'm sorry, Gab. It sucks that he can't be here to see his kid." Then Ella scratches her head. "If I remember from my sonograms, Gracie was so much bigger at five months."

Gabby sits up straight.

"Ms. Matthews..." says the doctor.

"I'm going to be sick. We're finished, right?" She holds her head in her hands and exhales hard. Ella, can you wait outside, please?"

"Sure, I'll be in the waiting room. You okay?"

"We'll take care of this. Thank you." The doctor opens the door for Ella to exit.

With Ella out of earshot and the door closed, Dr. Black looks at Gabby with a furrowed brow.

"You seem upset. What's going on?"

Gabby lies back down on the examining table. "How many weeks along am I?"

"I would say from the dates you gave us and the size of the fetus, about thirteen weeks. Is something wrong? Your friend seems to think you are further along."

"It's complicated."

"Yes, I heard you lost your husband. This must be very difficult." Dr. Black cleans the gel off Gabby's stomach.

"Ella thinks the baby is my husband's...he was in a coma for the past four months."

"So, the baby isn't his?"

"No."

"What are you going to tell your friend?"

"I could lie and say that I had his sperm aspirated and that I had invitro."

"You could. That's plausible. But you would have to continue that story. Is that what you want?" The doctor turns to input data into the computer.

Gabby places her pink shift over her head. "What would you do?"

"What you tell others is your business. My job is to make sure that this baby is born healthy. You do want this baby, right?"

"I guess...I'm not sure." She turns and asks the doctor to button the back of her dress.

Dr. Black turns her around and places her hands on her shoulders. "Gabby, we need to have a serious discussion. You're already past the first trimester, and if you don't want this baby, time is running short. What's going on?"

"It's been awful these past few months."

"Here, sit down and tell me everything. I can't imagine having a spouse die."

"One night, just one night, ...I needed to feel something. Every day I cared for my husband, praying that he would wake up. I loved him, and it was so hard to watch him slip further and further away." She takes a deep breath. "Then, one evening, my old boyfriend knocks on the door. He brought wine, we talked and laughed, and it felt nice. It felt normal. I needed to escape from my life. He kissed me, and I didn't stop him. Can you understand?"

"Gabby, I'm not here to judge."

"Does this man know he's the father?"

"Yes, but I didn't tell him. One of the nursing staff found the pregnancy test in the trash and felt it her duty to share."

"What does he think?"

"I haven't asked him."

"You haven't discussed it...I see." The doctor taps her pen on her palm. "You asked for my advice, so here it is. First, I would ask myself if I wanted this baby. If the answer is no, then we need to make a different plan. But if the answer is yes, then I would definitely have a conversation with the father. From my experience, things go better if both parties are involved."

Gabby picks at her fingernails. "You're right. He has wanted to talk, but I've pushed him away. My husband's death… has taken over everything."

"I can understand why you're confused. You've been dealing with things that no one should have to deal with. Your family wants to help you. I would let them. Do you want this baby?" Dr. Black stands.

"Yes."

"Then talk with the father. Here is your prescription for prenatal vitamins. Make an appointment for next month, and, Gabby…I'm really sorry for your loss. Please keep your appointments with Carole. Talking with a therapist can give great insights." She opens the door. "Any other questions?"

Gabby shakes her head. "Thank you."

CHAPTER 19

A few days later, the congregation exits the First Methodist Church after Sunday service, the sun high overhead. The church, originally a mission built of local white Texas limestone, is in the center of the small town of Midway. The town got its name because it's directly halfway between the larger towns on the north/south route of one of the few two-lane highways. The church boasts housing some of the men who fought in the Battle of the Alamo, including Davy Crockett, before they gave their lives.

The King family, Ella, Will, and their daughter, Gracie Anna, wait inside. Gracie's private baptism is scheduled for this Sunday's regular service. Gabby, wearing a high-waisted blue chiffon dress, stands on the church steps in four-inch stilettos. Unaccustomed to wearing heels, she shifts her weight, waiting for Stan and Marie's arrival. Parishioners pass by, some offering small talk and farewell waves. As she waits, her wish is to face the sun and have it flood warmth into her cold soul.

In the meantime, Richard exits the arched front doors and descends, heading in her direction. It's been about two weeks since they had lunch with Steve Prime.

"You look nice," Richard says. "Blue's a good color on you."

Her chiffon dress has a full skirt to hide her enlarging abdomen.

She jumps at the sound of his voice. "It matches my mood. I'm surprised you're here—Richard Wright attending church. Nope, I can't recall that ever happening. Is this a first?" If she were a smoker, she would be sure to light one up.

"Your father thought that some photos snapped in a church would help my image. I was here for the 11:00 a.m. service, checking off another of your father's planned appointments."

"You are my daddy's main boy." She looks away.

"That's not quite fair, Gabby." He scratches the back of his head. "So, you and Uncle Stan are going to be Gracie's godparents. Makes sense since you and Ella have been best friends forever and Stan being Will's brother."

He looks down at his shoes. "Since I'm already here, I'll stay. Is that all right with you?"

With a shrug of her shoulders, she asks, "Shouldn't you seek my daddy for an answer?" She reads the hurt on his face.

"Okay then, with no objection from you, I think I'll make my own decision…and stay."

"Suit yourself." She turns away to face the parking lot.

He rubs his hands together. "I've been concerned about you. How are you feeling?"

She holds his eyes but only for a brief second. "Fine."

"Any morning sickness?"

"A bit, but not too much." She bites her lip and pushes a loose strand of blond hair behind her ear. His puppy dog eyes dump waves of guilt, which make her ponder. When did she become so cynical? Life has handed her a hard knock, but taking it out on this man before she enters God's sacred house compels her to feel like a hypocrite.

"Richard, I'm sorry." Her hand blocks the sun from her eyes. "Maybe later we can talk?"

He beams. "Sure, I would like that. I would like that."

"Thanks. After the baptism, everyone's coming to the ranch for lunch."

"Is this an invitation?" He smiles. "Lunch at your ranch was not on my schedule, but I'll work it in." He chuckles.

A jeep pulling into the parking lot interrupts their conversation. Stan and Marie hop out. Marie's long dark hair glistens in the sunlight. Stan's quick to grab her hand.

After climbing the church steps, Marie stands to the side as Stan brings Gabby in for a hug. "Howdy, sis."

Ever since Stan started dating Marie, he has been calling Gabby by this nickname. Richard keeps his distance.

"Hi, Gabby. It's a big day. Hi, Richard. Surprised to see you here." Marie has her phone out. "Stan and Gabby, get close for a pic. The godparents." She giggles.

After posing, Gabby asks, "How's work at the horse center? I miss it. I hope to start back on Monday."

"We've missed you too. Everything's going well—the veterans are doing their part, we have lots of clients, and the weather's been good."

"Thanks for taking care of things."

"It's the least we can do." He looks at the time. "Hey, we should go. We have a baptism to attend."

Marie and Stan head off. Gabby turns to Richard. "Time to go. I've never been a godmother before."

"You'll make a great godmother—pretty, too." He grins from ear to ear and holds out his arm.

She rolls her eyes and shakes her head, but he stands there waiting with his arm extended.

"Shall we?"

Reluctantly, she takes hold of his hand, and they enter the church together.

CHAPTER 20

G abby beholds the light shining through the stained-glass window, leaving a rainbow of reflections on the nearby pew. The organist has stayed to play for the private baptism, the soft notes drifting in the air like sweet incense. In her lap sleeps the quiet angel that will be welcomed into the family of believers. Gabby, an only child who lived on the ranch away from other families, hasn't had much experience with babies. There was no babysitting to fill the evenings during her teenage years.

She's a bit afraid of the bundle she holds, but that's not why her hands tremble. In contrast to her calm surroundings, her thoughts fly like incoming missiles launched from all directions. She's trying to use the positive feedback methods she's learned in her therapy sessions to still her racing heart. It's not working. Unable to flee, she fears a panic attack will certainly ensue.

Closing her eyes, she takes deep breaths and then focuses her attention on the large wooden cross that hangs suspended from the vaulted ceiling. The caption for a vestibule photo said that this oak cross was added after the original gold one, which sat on the altar for over a hundred years, was stolen. The new cross has been sanded to round the edges, offering a softness—as opposed to the description of the old, rugged cross from the song she learned in her early years. The cross is a symbol of forgiveness, a symbol of new life, and a symbol of grace.

The calm innocence of the sleeping Gracie, cradled in her arms, penetrates her soul. She is confronted with the newfound enlightenment that God will forgive her, if only she would ask. Suddenly it occurs to her that she has allowed anger to overtake her so much that now she's unable to offer love to anyone, and clearly not even to this tiny person who's to become her godchild.

Why, oh why, God, did you take Brett? her silent prayer pleads. Then, words spoken as if by Brett himself, whisper in her ear, "There are no guarantees, my love. Isn't it better to have loved and lost than to have never loved at all?" She bites the inside of her cheek. Didn't Richard use these same words?

Brett would wish her to be happy. She remembers when she escaped to Washington D.C. and how Brett came after her, professing to love her, even her faults, rather than lose her. She's lucky to have found a love so rich and pure. Isn't God's love greater?

If God can forgive her, and Brett can forgive her, then why is it so hard to forgive herself? Lashing out at Richard is juvenile. He had nothing to do with Brett's death, and she willingly consented to have sex with him. So why is she punishing him? Could it be that she's releasing her anger and wants him to share her guilt because it makes her feel better about herself?

Night after night, she prayed and hoped that if she believed enough, Brett would wake up. When signs of his deterioration began, she ignored them. When the seizures started, his condition degraded rapidly. That's when she grasped that his recovery wasn't in their future. She can't count the numerous times that she thought about taking her life. The afternoon when she started researching drugs in preparation for her husband's mercy killing and her suicide, Richard came knocking at her door. It was the first time he had visited since Brett's accident, exactly two months later. Was it fate?

In the month it took her to sneak enough drugs and gain her nerve to carry out her plan, she discovered she was pregnant. Now, if she proceeds, she will also be taking an innocent life. Richard has given her a reason to live. Instead of a cloak of shame, this pregnancy is a life-saving gift. And it's her life that is being saved.

With the knowledge of the pregnancy, her plans were halted, and she'll never know if she would have been brave enough to carry out the modern-day Romeo and Juliet scenario.

She's also alive today because Rita and Jamie took her under their wings after Brett's passing. She's uncertain whose idea it was for them to insist that she live at the ranch. However, both women blame it on her daddy.

Two days after Brett passed, they came to her house and used their key when she didn't answer the door.

After hearing all of the noise, a weepy-eyed, hungover Gabby stood in the hall. "What are you doing here?"

"We're moving you to the main house." Jamie's head was in her refrigerator, unloading food into a cooler.

"This is my house and where I live."

"That it is, but right now, you're coming to live with us."

"I have things to do."

"Make a list. We'll be sure everything gets done."

"But...

"It's for the best. Your daddy wants you with us. When your daddy makes up his mind, it's as good as set in stone." Rita closed the kitchen pantry. "You can take it up with him tonight at dinner."

"But...you can't do this?"

Rita placed her arm around Gabby. "We can do this. You've been through something terrible. We're your family, and we love you. Families lean on each other in difficult times. Families help you get through it. Let us help you, please, honey. Do it for you. Do it for the baby!"

She was too drained physically and emotionally to resist. In the subsequent weeks, the extent of their care was intense. It was as though she was in a boarding school or jail. Every day they followed a schedule. There were scheduled walks, scheduled meals, scheduled rest time, and scheduled chores. Carole, her therapist, made house visits three times a week. She was given pills: vitamins, antidepressants, and a sleeping pill each night. And yes, they made sure that she swallowed them.

As she thinks back over those weeks, some days seemed to have blended together, and many days were a blur as she vaguely recalls going through the motions. One day, in particular, she remembers sitting in a shower chair while Jamie lathered soap over her body. It's shocking when a flashback like that pops into her mind. Apparently, she will never remember the full extent of her depression.

After a week under their care, she started feeling different. It wasn't like she was back to her normal self because she'll be forever changed after losing her love. But it was as though a dark curtain was slowly lifting. Still, first thing in the morning, they'd knock at her bedroom door to get her moving, even though she wished to pull the covers over her head and stay there. They monitored her food intake, and many times during these past weeks, she's shoveled food down her throat merely to stop their nagging as they advocated for the welfare of her unborn child. She could tell by how her clothes fit that she was gaining back some of the weight she had lost.

Today, she still lives in the main house in her former bedroom. She's not ready to go back to her house and face the emptiness and the memories.

She feels a nudge on her shoulder, bringing her back to the present, and notices everyone standing. With Gracie still in her arms, Richard helps her to her feet and ushers her out of the pew to the baptismal font with Stan and the proud parents. Ella's dressed in a navy-blue floral print, which shows off her figure that she boasts is back to her pre-pregnancy size. At six foot two, Will stands to her right, wearing a gray suit with a pocket square made from the same print as Ella's dress. Gabby thinks they model the perfect family.

The minister raises his right hand and reads from the open Bible. Little Gracie is baptized with holy water in the name of the trinity—the father, the son, and the holy spirit. In her quiet voice, which contrasts Stan's deep one, together they vow to help raise the baby girl in the lacy white dress nestling in her arms. After the promise is sealed with prayers and benediction, she looks down into the angelic face of her goddaughter, and a warm love washes over her.

She's beginning to come to terms with her past and accepts the symbol of the cross hanging above. It reminds her that Christ covers her sin. The heavy chain of guilt and the cold ball of grief that have threatened to destroy her lies dormant at her feet. For the first time in a long time, her smile is spontaneous. Today, God has given her love to share with Gracie and the child she carries in her womb.

CHAPTER 21

B ack at the ranch, the King and Adams families continue the celebration with a late lunch. Jamie, with Rita by her side, worked tirelessly the day before to prepare for the celebration. The men got involved too. Before leaving for church, Rusty had fired up the smoker, and several tri-tip roasts, marinated with the family recipe, have been slowly cooking for the past few hours. The meal will also include a crock of baked beans, homemade potato salad, coleslaw, and Jamie's popular baked honey-wheat bread. It is a typical barbeque menu served with onions, pickles, and, of course, hot and spicy barbeque sauce.

"What can I do to help?" Ella asks.

"You can pour water in the glasses. Hey, where's Gracie?" Gabby says, looking up from making the peach cobbler to be served with ice cream for dessert.

"I fed her, and now she's out on the porch with Will and Stan. Will's such a good father."

"I can tell by the way he looks at her that he loves her. You and Will made a beautiful child. Are you going to have another?"

"Not just yet, but eventually. Someday in the not-so-distant future." She pours water into another glass. "We're really looking forward to this lunch. We've been craving authentic Texas barbeque since we got here. There aren't any good barbeque restaurants in D.C. Well, not that we've found anyway."

As Gabby waits for the meat to be taken out of the smoker, she walks out the back door and sees Richard alone in the garden.

"Hey," she calls, walking toward him.

"Hey yourself. Lunch ready?" He stands straighter, chewing on a blade of grass. She gasps as she realizes Brett used to do the same. It takes her by surprise.

"Not yet, but soon. Can we talk?"

He leans over, picks a yellow flower from the garden, twirls it between his fingers, and then places it behind her ear. "Sure, I'd really like that."

There's a sadness behind his dark eyes.

"I'm sorry I've been evasive and ...not very pleasant, especially when it comes to you."

"You have a lot going on."

"Thanks for giving me an excuse. After going to church today and having Gracie baptized, I got to thinking about our baby and about us." She rubs her hand over her swollen abdomen. "I do want you to be part of this child's life. Every child should have a father."

His face brightens. "I would like that too." He steps around the sunflowers to get closer.

"Glad we agree on that."

134

"Yes, of course. I'd like to spend more time with you now before the baby comes."

"Richard, I'm still dealing with Brett's death. It's too soon."

His smile fades, and he looks down.

"I'm sorry. I sense that's not what you want to hear. I still haven't been able to go back to my house." She looks over the field where she can see the roof of her home. "It would be best if I made peace with all of this before trying to start something new."

His head is still lowered. He avoids looking at her.

"Richard, I'm turning that idea down today, but how about a raincheck? Please ask me again."

"Okay, that's fair enough."

The sound of the old brass bell on the porch gets their attention.

"Lunch is on. Let's go get some of the best BBQ in Texas." She reaches for his hand, and they walk side by side back to the house.

CHAPTER 22

"Gabby, Richard, in my office." King's tone alerts that this is business, not part of the friendly gathering.

It seems the relaxed atmosphere present during lunch is over. Gabby looks at Richard before her daddy and then bites her upper lip as she stands.

With the office door closed behind them, King offers Richard a glass of bourbon. Richard checks out the bottle. "Garrison Brother's Cowboy. This is good stuff."

She wonders if she has misread her daddy's tone, and they have been called into the office to celebrate. Or is this expensive bourbon meant to dampen the sting of bad news?

"We've got a lot to consider going forward. Princess, I'm sorry I can't give you more time. Time is moving along, and we, the three of us in this room, need to be united and consistent in our actions and words. There is more at stake in the next year, something bigger than your agendas. The whole state of Texas is on the line." King clicks his glass on Richard's before taking a swig.

"First, I want to thank my beautiful daughter for reeling in the biggest donation and visible supporter into our camp thus far. Steven Prime has great influence and a large wallet. Princess, you did good." He lifts his glass.

"You sure did," Richard says and lifts his glass to click with King's.

She nods in appreciation of their praise. "Glad I could help. He seems like a good ol' Texan. It wasn't that hard."

"I think you appearing so distraught was the real key. He likes the idea of being able to rescue a woman in distress. And he liked the idea that Richard immediately jumped to help because he could see himself in Richard's actions. At the time, I thought the move was risky. It was a make-or-break situation, but it worked in our favor." King sits behind his desk. "Now, down to the serious issue—this baby. Gabby, you may wish to take a seat.

I couldn't be more thrilled to have another grandchild on the way. Little Gracie is cute as a button, but she's not a King. We have quite a complication here, but it can work to our advantage if we play our cards right. Everyone will need to make sacrifices." He turns to Gabby.

"Few folks know that this baby isn't Brett's, and for now, we're going to keep it that way. Voters can be turned off with a candidate who sleeps with another man's wife." He holds up his hand. "It doesn't matter the circumstances. For the voter, it's black and white. With that said, Gabby, sweetheart, you need time to process the ordeal you've been through. Most voters expect a widow to grieve for at least a year, if not more. You'll be giving birth around February, just eight months before the polls open, which means that your baby will be born with you as a single parent. Understand?"

She nods but doesn't speak, even though she has a million questions she wants to blurt out.

Next, he turns to Richard. "You will be on the campaign trail. You will be spending day and night winning votes. There will be days when you'll think you can't shake another hand, walk another step, or give another speech. Trust me. It's brutal." King stands and faces the window, his back to them.

"I understand that this is your first child, and you want to be a father and act like a father. However, you cannot. There will be no handholding. Your undivided attention is the campaign trail. You know firsthand how careful we need to be, especially since you reported that we have already had a journalist sneaking around and asking questions and that we've had drones taking photos over this ranch."

She sits up straighter and raises her eyebrows.

"We cannot afford a scandal. Am I making myself clear?" He faces them and points a finger. "You're both aware of the high stakes. Let's be smart. So, Richard, you will not be visiting Gabby, especially not at her house and never alone. For example, here, inside this house is a safe place. At a restaurant alone in the city—not okay. We need to be smart, focused." He paces back and forth. "The more advanced Gabby's pregnancy gets, the more she may wish to be with you and want you to share in the amazing birthing process. Sorry to be the bearer of bad news, but in this case, Richard will not be allowed at the birth. He will not be allowed at the hospital. Gabby, pick someone else as your significant other because it's not going to be Richard."

King rubs his head and stares Richard down. "I know you will be anxious to hold your son or daughter. You'll be able to do that, but not at the hospital and certainly away from the cameras. On the campaign trail, you'll be a celebrity, so you'll need to think like a celebrity." He stops speaking and swirls the bourbon in his glass. "Let's go over this again, one step at a time. First, you cannot be seen together alone. After the baby is born, you will still need to be separated. You'll share the joys of parenthood in private, away from the press, journalists, and cameras. You may be asking, what about the long-term? That's too far in the future. " He looks from one blank face to the other. "Any questions?"

Richard is the first to leap into the obvious. "What if we tell the truth?"

Gabby sits on the edge of her seat.

"The truth… are you kidding? I already mentioned that the voters would not understand. You'll lose the race. They'll look at you as a playboy without morals. Is that what you want? If you're willing to give up that easily, maybe you aren't hungry enough to be the next governor. These are simple, clear-cut guidelines. If both of you play it this way for the next year or so, then, if warranted, Richard can officially adopt the child. Whatever you both decide."

"Wait, adopt my own kid?" Richard throws his hands up in the air.

King chuckles. "There's no way your name's going on that birth certificate. That would be the dumbest thing we could do. We may as well open a window and broadcast it to the world."

Gabby sits speechless, trying to understand her daddy's rules and Richard's outrage.

Her daddy addresses her. "Gabby, do you have any questions? I know this will be tough without Richard's support, but it's what we have to do to get to where we want to go. We've worked years for this. We are on the homestretch. Stick to the guidelines, and a year will pass quickly."

Gabby's voice is deliberate as though thinking aloud. "I never thought it would go down like this. Richard can't even see his own child the first few days of its life? Isn't there another way?"

"Sorry, Princess. It's the only way. This is a delicate situation, and this is what we have to do to fix it." He drains his bourbon. "I need some fresh air. Both of you, take some time to get used to the idea. I'll give you a moment." He exits and closes the door behind him.

"Okay, guess we've been told. I don't like it." Richard paces in front of the desk.

"Daddy seems pretty set that this is what we have to do. I guess he's right. People won't understand and ..." She lowers her head and takes a deep breath to finish her sentence. "What were we thinking? At least we could have had protected sex. I could ruin your career."

"Hey, stop that." He kneels at her feet. "I'm not sorry, not in the least. Everything will be all right. We can do this."

"You'll miss the birth. You'll miss the first two days. You can't get those things back."

"I'll be the next governor. It's what I've been working for. All of this will blow over. We can do this. We have to."

He reaches up to kiss her, but she turns her face and stands.

"I can't." After opening the door, she turns to face him. "It's not right."

Standing in the office alone, he wonders what his future will hold.

CHAPTER 23

Hey, Gabby, come here. Gracie's awake. Let's get a family photo on the porch. Richard, can you take the pic?" Stan says, waving his arms. "Let's go, everyone."

Richard looks around at the family. It's true, he's an outsider, but so is Marie. However, Marie takes part and starts to position the family in an orderly fashion. Rita and King sit with Gracie on Rita's lap. Will and Ella stand, one on each side. Last, Gabby and Stan stand side-by-side behind the seated grandparents. Even Ryder, Stan's dog, earns a spot with the family. He snaps several photos of them: the happy parents, the proud grandparents holding their first grandchild, and yes, the godparents and the dog. A pain gnaws at his gut as he churns on King's words that his name won't be on the birth certificate and that he'll miss the birth of his first child. It doesn't seem fair.

Stan stays out on the porch after the others have gone inside. Gabby rocks on the chair, and he takes the rocker next to hers. Ryder rests by his side.

"How are you holding up? You seem quiet."

"It's been a long day. I guess I'm tired."

"We're godparents. Do you think we should make a plan?"

She's confused. "What kind of a plan?"

"A plan so that we're prepared…in case something happens."

"I don't think Will and Ella are going anywhere." She chuckles and gives Ryder a pat on his head. "I'll Google to see if there are any books written about the responsibilities of godparents. Maybe that would help."

"That's a great idea, Gab." His eyes dance. "Why didn't I think of that?"

She laughs. "I was joking."

"Oh…"

"Stan, relax." She pats his hand. "It's sweet that you're taking the job of being a godparent seriously. Maybe you could be my baby's godfather too."

He looks as though a cat got his tongue.

"It's okay, Stan. We can talk about it."

His perplexed expression astonishes her. "Oh my God, you didn't know." She covers her mouth with her hand. "I'm so sorry."

"You're pregnant?" He looks at her stomach.

"Yep."

"Wow, that's great. How far along are you?"

"A few months." She wants to be vague.

"Knowing that a part of Brett will be with you must be comforting."

She bites her lip. She hates lying to Stan, but after the talk with her daddy, she feels that she must. She looks straight ahead rather than tell a lie.

"Congratulations."

"Thank you. I'm still getting used to the idea. It came as quite a shock."

"You had a lot of things on your plate, big things. During all that, you never asked for help. You know I would have been there for you."

"You have been running the equine therapy program and managing the vets. You and Marie have been great. That's where you need to be. I'm very grateful both of you are there to run the center."

"That's our job, silly. Hey, I live right down the lane." He points in the direction of his house. "I could be there in two minutes or less. Ask for help, okay?"

"I'll remember that in the future."

He sits forward in his chair. "Were you serious about me being the godfather?"

She laughs again, and this time it's a hardy laugh. "Could be. You think you're up for it? I'd hate to send you over the edge."

"I'm tougher than you think." He winks.

"Let's take this one child at a time. We've got until February to figure it all out." She looks at him. "Enough about me. How's it going between you and Marie?"

"It's going well. Really good, maybe too good." He rubs his hands together.

"Tell me about that." She's eager to learn more.

"This relationship is going fast."

"You're older, and you know what you want."

"True, but Marie's only twenty-four. I remember thinking I knew everything at that age. Boy, was I wrong. I didn't know jack shit."

"Now, you are a wise old man at thirty-four."

He isn't sure if she's being sarcastic.

"I'll be thirty-five in a few months."

"Have you two talked about the future? She came here to be with you. That should mean something."

"True again, and it was her idea that we move in together."

"My advice would be to ride the wave. Living together and working together is a lot of togetherness. Let your relationship take its course. Is she pushing you for a bigger commitment?"

He rubs his forehead. "Not exactly in those words. But I get the feeling that she wants more. I think she needs time to process the kidnapping she went through this spring. I don't want her mistaking gratitude for love."

"You saved her life, finding her the way you did. The odds are great that she would have died, but I hear it wasn't about the hero finding the human trafficking victim out in the desert that made her love you. It was more about the stargazing Romeo that clinched the deal."

He sits back in the rocking chair and raises his chin with amused interest. "Oh, really? What else did she say?"

"Something about a rendezvous in San Diego, but your head's already big enough. Besides, that's sacred girl talk. I would be breaking code if I told you more."

"So that's the way you're going to get around this, huh, sis?"

"You bet, bro." She twists a blond strand of hair around her finger. "Hey, Richard says that he wants Marie to give an account of her kidnapping ordeal at a special committee hearing on human trafficking in Washington, D.C. in two weeks. Is she up for it?"

"She's a little concerned—nervous is probably a better word."

"It will be good therapy for her to tell her story and have the gratification that she did something to keep others from falling into this trap. Please encourage her. Her testimony can make a difference, especially with congress appropriating funds. Isn't her girlfriend, Alexia, still in that mental institution?"

"Yes, and that's another sad story. It gets Marie down that she's unable to fix her friend. Maybe it's a bit of survivor's guilt. Heck, I'm no therapist."

"Her testimony can help Alexia as well. I'll be back at the horse center, so you can go with her to offer support. It could bring up some bad memories, and she may need you."

"I'd like that if you think you're ready… with the pregnancy and all."

"Many pregnant women work up until the day their babies are born. Stop worrying." She pats his hand. "Going back to work will be good for me. Probably better than hanging around here. Too many reminders."

"Have you been painting?"

"No, and I should have painted something for Ella to hang in Gracie's nursery. I didn't have the energy to paint, and my mind can't focus. That's why I'm hoping that going back to work will help."

"Of course you didn't feel like painting, but you will, in due time. In the past, painting seems to have helped you work through things. I've witnessed that."

"You're right. I should give it a try after Ella and Will leave."

Stan stands and holds out his hand to help her up. "It's been a long day. I'm going to round up Marie and head for home. You should rest as well. Come on, Ryder, let's go home."

The dog perks up his ears and barks as if he understands.

"Stan, don't tell Marie about me…the pregnancy, not just yet."

"Sure, if that's what you want."

He hugs her. "I'll let you tell her when you're ready."

CHAPTER 24

September

G abby descends the curved staircase into a quiet dining room. She walks into the kitchen to find Jamie wiping down the kitchen counters.

The room is empty. "Where is everyone?"

Jamie looks up from the counter she's cleaning. "Out and about. Let's see, Rita and King went into town. They'll drop Marie and Stan at the airport, then she'll spend the day at the art gallery, and your daddy has some business meetings with Richard. Seems he's taking a later flight. Here, have some coffee." She places a mug of steamy brown liquid across the counter.

"I forgot they were leaving so early." She sniffs the steam and embraces the warmth of the mug in her hands. "I need to get to the horse center."

"Stan said to tell you that he didn't schedule any appointments for this morning so that you can have a half-day."

"That was nice of him."

"He's a good man, that one. Rusty's out with the ranch hands rounding up calves. They're going to brand them and separate them from their mothers. Hope you got your earplugs because there won't be much sleep tonight."

"Thanks for the warning. Wow, life goes on." She casts her eyes down. "It's almost as if nothing has changed." Her voice breaks.

"I'm sorry, honey. Life does go on. The cattle will be branded, moved to different pastures, and then sold at market, just like they have been for a century. The sun will rise in the east and set in the west long after we're both gone." She stands next to Gabby. "I know how much it hurts. You miss him. We all do."

Gabby pouts. "It's not fair." The tears stream down her cheeks.

"Life is not fair. My mama told me that when I was a wee little one, and I see it happening all around. You're right. Life isn't fair. We need to make the best with the hand that we're dealt." Jamie pulls her in, and she lays her hand on her shoulder.

"What am I to do?"

Jamie strokes her hair. "My mama also told me that the best way to get over feeling sorry for yourself is to do something for others. There are lots of hurting people in this world. Find one of them and make a difference."

She looks to Jamie with her tear-filled eyes. "I said that same thing about Marie and her testimony to Congress. She should feel better making a difference, especially for her friend Alexia."

"You, girl, need to follow your own advice. What are you and that little one of yours craving for breakfast? You need a good meal if you're going to save someone today, and I make the best breakfast this side of Texas."

Gabby wipes her eyes and sniffles. "Blueberry pancakes?"

"I had a hunch that's what you'd say. The batter's in the fridge. Be ready in a jiffy."

CHAPTER 25

G abby unlocks the front door of the horse center and turns on the lights. There is a truck in the parking lot, so she knows at least one of the veterans is here to care for the horses. Even though Stan didn't schedule horse therapy appointments until noon, the horses still need to be fed, and their stalls need to be cleaned. She fills her lungs with air and closes her eyes, taking in the fresh smell of sweaty leather, fresh pine shavings, and hay. God, she's missed this. However, it is bittersweet because although these smells remind her of the important work she started here, they also remind her of her late husband. Several steps inside the door, and she's crying. She promised to be strong; that's not happening.

She swore that she was ready. She had taken the first step by encouraging Stan to be with Marie for the trip to Washington. Who's here to support her? No Stan and no Brett. Kneeling alone, she feels despair as a huge wave of abandonment floods over her. She gasps for air as if she were on the verge of drowning. In talking to herself, she tries to gain insight. *It's okay. You're okay. Take some deep breaths. Pull yourself together. Soon patients will be coming through that door.* Her knees buckle, and she lies on the floor in a fetal position, whimpering.

She's not aware of the side door opening, but the sound of an uneven gait gets her attention. Gregg, the older veteran, is bending over her. The strain on his face suggests pain because when bending, he exerts more pressure on his prosthetic leg, a daily reminder of his past.

"Ms. King, Ms. King, are you all right? What should I do? Call 911?"

She's embarrassed for her outbreak. "No, please don't. I'm fine."

"With all due respect, anyone can see that you are not fine." With difficulty, he lowers to the ground and kneels next to her.

She senses that he has a kind soul as she forces herself to look at the weathered face, the understanding eyes. It's like they share a connection, even though no further words are spoken.

She wipes her eyes and fakes a smile. "Help me up."

"Sure can, ma'am."

It's a bit awkward; she should be the one assisting him to stand. To allow him his dignity, she's patient and respectful, lowering her eyes until he stands and then assists her.

She straightens her shirt and pulls it over her bulging stomach. He's staring, and now she's humiliated. Can this get any worse?

"I lost my husband."

"Yes, ma'am, I'm so sorry. We're all aware."

She reads empathy in his eyes. "Then you can understand that I'm not quite myself." She wipes her eyes.

"Yes, ma'am."

"Maybe it's sort of like when you came back from the war. You had to make peace with some things."

He nods. "I understand that, ma'am. Yes, I do."

"Okay, good. The death of my husband is like war. I'll be all right…really. Thanks for helping me up."

"Anytime, and congratulations."

"What?"

"Your condition." He turns away.

He's caught her off guard, and heat rises to the top of her head. "Oh, yes, thank you."

Suzanne, the temporary therapist, walks through the door and stops in her tracks, assessing the situation before her. She worked here filling in part-time before they brought Marie on board as their full-time equine therapist.

"Ma'am." Gregg tips his hat. "Holler if you need me. I'll be in the stables."

She acknowledges with a nod.

"Hi, Gabby, everything all right?" Suzanne asks.

"Yes, of course."

"You look like a zombie with that mascara under your eyes. You'll scare Austin and his little sister Maddie. They're our first appointment. I don't smell the coffee. You know I need that cup of Joe to get me through the afternoon."

She frowns. "Sorry, I should have gotten here earlier."

"Not a problem. I'm happy to make it."

"Thanks. Umm, Suzanne, thanks for telling me about the mascara." She uses both her index fingers to swipe the black from under her eyes.

Suzanne pops her head out the small kitchen doorway. "Anytime, Gab, anytime. Thanks for having me back. I'm glad you're back, too.

Sorry about Brett."

She rolls her eyes, then remembers her promise to be strong. She stands tall and squares her shoulders. Her day can only get better.

CHAPTER 26

Washington, D. C.

Marie and Stan are out on a stroll through the city after having a late dinner with Richard. On the flight, Marie had put pen to paper and answered some key questions about her human trafficking experience in preparation for the hearing. Richard wanted to curb her answers to steer the committee toward his proposed senate bill. The publicity for this hearing will be shared on all media, gaining him exposure for tackling human trafficking through funding.

"You really know your way around this city," Marie says. The hint of pride in her voice makes him feel special.

"I should. I lived here for eight years." He points to the Lincoln Memorial. "Isn't it beautiful? It's my favorite building. I like the way the lights show on the water. I lived in a condo just a few blocks to the left. I sold it when I started building the house at the ranch."

She takes his hand and swings it as they walk toward the reflecting pool. The calm evening makes the reflections clearly visible. "Lit up at night, these monuments are impressive. You never told me about the condo."

"It wasn't important. I decided to live in Texas before I met you. It was time to move on with my life."

"How did you know...when it was time?"

"How did you know to come to Texas and work at the equine center?"

"It was an opportunity."

"Explain."

"There was this job opening, and I heard that one of the owners was single and handsome, so I thought, why not give it a try?"

He stops walking and faces her. "Did you now?" he teases.

Her eyes sparkle. "Yes, something like that."

"Really...single and handsome. Not because of his stargazing expertise?"

Her face turns red. "Someone told you."

"I'll never tell."

She punches him in the shoulder. "You have a knack for fishing for compliments."

"It must be the lawyer in me."

"Do you miss it, being a lawyer? Living here in the city?"

"Nope, not in the least. Love the ranch and working with the horses."

"It suits you. You seem content."

He pulls her in for a kiss. "I'm very content, especially now that our new equine-assisted therapist seems to find me attractive enough to share living quarters."

"Oh, you wanted a roommate."

"To clarify, a special roommate, who comes with benefits."

"You're so bad."

"But I'm honest." He pulls on her arm. "Come on. You have a big day tomorrow."

"I'm nervous about that."

"You'll be fine."

"Stan, thanks for coming. It means a lot."

He smiles and walks with his arm around her.

CHAPTER 27

Early the following morning, Stan and Marie meet Richard on the Capitol steps. There is a drizzle of rain, so Richard holds out his umbrella to cover Marie.

"Our hearing will be conducted across the street at the Hart Building. This way." He ushers them down the sidewalk. "This is the newest and largest senate building, and my office is on the fourth floor."

After entering the large atrium, they face a monumental black steel and aluminum sculpture. Marie stops, and her eyes follow the immense structure.

"It's called 'Mountains and Clouds,'" Richard says.

"I get that...very appropriate. It's huge." She gives a nervous laugh.

"We'll take a tour of the building later. We need to get moving. Our hearing has been moved to the Central Hearing Facility on the second floor." There's excitement in his voice. "The article in *The Post* seems to have generated interest. This is our largest room. Having a large crowd is a good thing."

They make their way through security before taking the elevator to the second floor. The deputy opens the door to the large chamber and nods.

"You ready?"

Looking uneasy, she doesn't respond.

Richard says, "It's a bit intimidating. I remember how I felt when I first came here. You're going to be great. Just be yourself, and tell your story. If you have any concerns, look to me, and I'll ask for a break."

"How long do you think this will take?" she asks in a shaky voice.

Stan pulls Marie closer to him.

"It depends on how many questions the members ask. Two or three hours is my guess. I'll treat you to a fabulous lunch as a reward. Promise." He straightens his tie. "Thanks for doing this."

She takes Richard's hand. "I'm doing this for myself, for Alexia, and for all of the other victims out there."

"That's my girl. Tell them in the same way you are telling me now. Stan, these hearings are open to the public. You can sit here." He points to some chairs in the back of the room.

"I can't sit with Marie?"

"I'm afraid not. She'll be at the table in front, with me, of course."

"I'll be fine, Stan." She gives a tense smile and rubs his arm.

Richard touches her shoulder. "You'll do great. I'll make sure the senators stick to our agenda. This is the first time we've discussed human trafficking to this depth since the Victims of Trafficking and Violence Protection Act was passed in 2000. " He looks at his phone. "Let's get settled. I want to review some key points."

Stan watches Marie and Richard as they take their places at a large table set with microphones in the front of the room. Members of Congress are slowly filtering in and taking their seats, along with the press and others. It's showtime.

Stan observes Richard placing his hand on the small of Marie's back when the hearing is over. She smiles as they sit close, deep in conversation. Stan, anxious to talk with Marie, walks toward them, but the deputy stops him.

"Sorry, sir."

"The hearing is over."

"Sorry, sir. The public isn't allowed. Please stand back."

"Really?" He rolls his eyes, then tries to tame the green-eyed monster within. He pulls back his shoulders and stands straight. Failing to make eye contact with Marie, he checks his Rolex. She and Richard have been in deep discussion for over five minutes. He's reminded of the importance of this hearing and that her remarks were crucial for helping present and future victims of this horrific crime.

As he continues to keep an eye on them, an image of former President Clinton comes to mind. When Stan worked as a lawyer, he had an opportunity to meet the former president at a fundraiser. Richard seems to have that same persuasive charm. He hopes that the young and impressionable Marie knows not to fall for his antics. Since he came to Texas he's watched Richard's actions, and he's not a fan of him. Should he warn her?

Finally, Richard picks up his files. Marie turns and walks at a fast pace toward Stan. Her face reads that she's relieved the hearing is over.

"Hey, you did great!" He pulls her in for a hug. "I'm very proud of you."

"She was fantastic. It couldn't have gone better," Richard says. "We should get the funding. Come on. I want to show you my office. You can meet my staff and help share our good news."

CHAPTER 28

Texas

Gabby stumbles up the steps to the main house after a long afternoon at the horse center. Working did indeed take her mind off her problems because she's more focused on removing her boots to relieve her aching feet.

"How was work?" Rita says, looking up from her magazine.

"Exhausting. It was only a half-day, and I'm having trouble imagining a full day tomorrow." She has successfully removed one boot and is pulling off the second.

"Suzanne was there, right?"

Gabby runs her fingers through her hair. "She's a rock. She was great."

"Good, I'm glad there is someone familiar with the center."

"I wish Stan and Marie were back."

"They'll be back tomorrow evening." Rita takes off her glasses. "They called a while ago. The hearing went better than expected. Stan says Marie was awesome. The press interviewed her and Richard after the hearing. They're off to some fancy restaurant—Richard's treat. Amanda's going to celebrate with them. You remember her?"

"Yes, I met her at our wedding." Her eyes cast downward, and she rubs her forehead. "I'm beat. I didn't realize that I'm so out of shape."

"Don't forget you're pregnant. That takes energy."

"How can I forget? I can't zip up my jeans." She lifts her shirt. "I never thought to get my maternity clothes from the house." She bites her lip. "I have some leftover from Jacob. After dinner, I should go home."

Rita stands. "I can get them. Tell me where they are."

"No, I should go."

"I don't want you in that house alone. It's too soon. Promise me you'll check with your doctor. Please call Carole and get her advice before going."

Gabby looks out the window and over the roof to the house that she built. Maybe Rita is right. After what happened today at the horse center, she probably can't handle going to the house, their house, filled with Brett's clothing and his scent. Will she ever be ready?

"Jamie and I will go tonight after dinner, and that's final. Besides, with Stan gone, Ryder needs a walk. You look beat, Gabby. You had a physically demanding day, and you don't need to tear yourself apart emotionally. Certainly not tonight."

Gabby fights back her tears.

"Oh, honey. I'm sorry." Rita hugs her. "You did well today. Let's get dinner, then you can take a nice bath, and I'll get your maternity clothes. Okay?"

She sniffles and nods, and then her eyes open wide. What was that? The slight flutter in her abdomen is her baby announcing that she's not alone. Her little one will help her get through this.

CHAPTER 29

The Next Day

Dinner at the King ranch is always a time of family and fellowship. Wayne King keeps it that way by telling a joke or a story, especially if the banter needs some spark. This evening the table will be full since Stan and Marie are back from D.C. Jamie has been slaving in the kitchen, making Stan's favorite pot roast and finishing it off with lemon meringue pie. Rita's been helping her but is excited to hear about Marie and her son's adventure. Gabby has yet to join in the cocktail hour since she went straight to her room to shower after work.

King and Rusty are in good spirits and sip on the special G.B. Cowboy bourbon, also celebrating that the cattle at the Fort Worth auction sold for a great price. To most, it would seem as though everything's back to normal. Almost as normal as the sun setting in the west, casting large shadows across the fields.

The room is lively with conversation as Gabby descends the curved stairway. Out of habit, her eyes search for her husband's familiar face. Realizing her error, she bites her nails. She forces a smile to return Marie's wide, welcoming one.

"Gabby, we missed you," Marie says, pulling away from Stan's side. "Thanks for helping Suzanne at the horse center. She says it went extremely well."

"Suzanne is great, and it helps that she's familiar with the center and the routine. Tell me all about the hearing."

"I can do better than that. Let me show you." Marie holds up a copy of *The Texas Sun's* front page. Under the headline, *Senator Wright's Bill to Secure Funding for Human Trafficking Victims,* is a photograph of Richard sporting a wide smile with Marie close at his side. Slightly behind them stand Amanda and Stan.

"I'll need to read the article, but you seem happy with the coverage. Congratulations."

"Thank you. It was nerve-racking but worth it. Now I feel empowered, knowing that I did something to help others, especially my friend Alexa. Throughout the whole ordeal, Richard was great. He was so nice and took care of everything. He made it easier than I thought it would be. And I met Amanda, who seems nice. She says she knows you."

"Yes, we've met."

"She's really smart, and I love the way she dresses. Her style is modern but classic. She and Richard make a good couple. I'm happy for them."

"Why is that...that you're happy for them?"

"When Richard was here after Gracie's baptism, he seemed out of sorts, like he was lonely or lost. As a therapist, I tried to get him to talk, but he just clammed up. I think it would be nice if he had someone…you know, a girlfriend. I don't see how someone with his looks, job, and political success could possibly be alone. In Washington, he was different. He was confident and in his element. He seemed happy."

"Really? That's interesting." Gabby pours sparkling water from the bar into her glass.

"He deserves to be happy, don't you agree?"

"Everyone deserves to be happy," she quips. "Excuse me. I need to speak with Rita."

She walks toward the kitchen and stops in the hallway to simmer over Marie's remark. She's certain that her comments are innocent. However, it is true that Richard was out of sorts that Sunday after her daddy had laid out the rules governing their future interactions. Later that evening, she had overheard them arguing, and from what she got from her eavesdropping, Richard was advocating for his name to be on the birth certificate. The voices got louder, and shortly thereafter, Richard left without saying goodbye.

Richard's career is at stake, and her daddy's wisdom is key, so it's best for now that they adhere to his plan. At the moment, she's grateful for today and unable to think about the future. In comparison, a few weeks ago, she wasn't even able to bathe herself, so it's just short of a miracle that she's worked these past two days at the equine-assisted therapy center. Work has given her a reason to exist, a reason to get out of bed in the morning and put one foot in front of the other when she'd rather pull the covers over her head and die. Brett's unforeseen death has been monumental, but she's still breathing and alive, and this, in itself, is a victory.

After dinner, she walks to the stable to spend time with her horse, as she and Brett had done many evenings before. And in her familiar habit, she looks up to the sky and offers a prayer, then wonders if Brett can wish on that same evening star. God knows how much she misses him, and she has yet to figure out how she will live without him.

Tomorrow is light-years away, but for today, she's surviving on one breath, taking one moment at a time. For the sake of her child, she puts one foot in front of another, going forward, although she continues to look back at what she's lost.

She glances over the field to the roof of her house. The setting sun leaves an orange glow reflecting off the tin. That house, full of memories, will keep standing, and someday she'll need to walk up the steps and open the front door to face the demons that lie within.

CHAPTER 30

The following morning, she says goodbye to Rita and Jamie, walks out the front door, and gets in her car, like she's done the past two days. But today, the Equine Center will not be her destination. She left a message with Stan and Marie, telling them that she would not be at work because she has an appointment, which, in part, is true. She does have an appointment with Carole, her psychologist, later this afternoon. Instead of meeting at her office, she asked Carole to come to her house. Carole agreed, stating that it would have to be her last appointment of the day, so she'll bring dinner.

Rather than agonize over the idea of returning to the house she built for herself and Brett, she woke up this morning deciding that the sooner, the better. Why not today? Do it, and stop the fretting. As usual, she pulls out of the circular drive, but instead of turning right to head for the road, she turns left and drives slowly down the gravel lane, trying not to draw any attention by stirring up dust, and heads for her house.

Once there, she clicks the garage door opener and waits for the door to rise. She plans to park in the garage so that there's no evidence that she is there. Like a sacred rite of passage, she needs to confront her past on her own terms.

Brett's accident caused a chasm, changing everything in a split second. Over the past few months, she has tried to transition into a new normal. When her daddy intervened, she lost control, and then fate struck, and Brett died. Following his death, the love from her family would not allow her to stay in her depressed state, and she survived. But surviving isn't living. Surviving is breathing and having a heartbeat. But feeling alive is what living is all about. She needs to reconcile and understand so that she'll be able to move forward again. She must do this. If not for herself, she'll do it for the life she carries.

Today, going home will be tough; she'll remember the good times and ache for more. She'll cry and plead with God to save her. She needs to understand what it means to be on her own. Who is Gabby King? She needs to define her purpose, form a new identity so she can reach a resolution.

Pulling the car into the garage, she meets her first challenge. She's forgotten that Brett's red sports car would be here. His car hasn't been driven in months. The battery is probably dead. She takes a breath and blows it out slowly, reminding herself that she can do this. This car holds many fond memories. She sweeps her hand over the smooth curve of the fender in the same way that she observed Brett do a million times. He loved this car. She reaches for the chain around her neck and slides his wedding ring back and forth, whispering a prayer.

At the front door, her hand trembles, making it difficult to get the key in the lock. As she opens the door, she is prepared for the beep of the alarm. Instead, she's met with silence. All of the shades are pulled, so the house is dark, and the smell is musty. On the foyer entryway table, she picks up a framed picture of their wedding day. The woman's eyes shine in her pink lace gown, and the man is dashing in his tux, a deep dimple piercing his smile. God, they had no idea how short their time together would be. If they had known, would they have done anything differently?

Her finger traces the outline of their faces, and a wet drop falls onto the glass. Her heart sinks to her gut, and she screams her anger. "Why did you get on that bull? It was a stupid thing to do...so stupid. We had it all. We were so great, and then, I had to watch you die." She throws the frame to the stone floor, and the glass shatters. She reaches over to pick it up, and blinded by her tears, she cuts her finger on the broken shards. As she sobs, she cries, "I kept you here, in our home. I tried to get you to wake up. I begged you to come back to me. I loved you. I still love you. Why did you leave me?"

She runs to his closet and buries her nose in his clothes, inhaling his familiar scent. She has missed this over the past few weeks. God, she misses him. But he's gone. She recalls how his arms wrapped around her, how he nuzzled her neck, and how she would wrap her finger around his brown curls. Reaching for the remote on her dresser, she tunes in to their favorite playlist. She closes her eyes and sways to the music, remembering:

It was the Valentine's ball at the country club. She was out on the porch, taking in some fresh air. He met her there, and his eyes sparkled when he asked her to dance. And as they swayed to the music, she was intoxicated by his essence. As his lips touched hers, she was left breathless. Their eyes told the story of that magical moment. She didn't intend to fall for him. He was the tennis professional at her country club. He had the reputation of a bad boy. She was the classy daughter of a wealthy oilman. Some things, such as why we love or who we love, can't be explained.

They were such opposites. Brett was carefree and always had a smile. He lived in the moment. She, on the other hand, made plans and contemplated the different angles of situations, tried to antici-pate outcomes. She was reserved and careful. She can understand how Brett's personality allowed him to get caught up in the moment, how he came to ride that bull. He was spontaneous and impulsive and thought himself invincible. Now, he's gone.

On the dresser next to the remote lies Brett's wallet. Upon open-ing it, she finds a photo, Brett's selfie of them on Rita and her daddy's wedding day. She traces his outline with her finger in an attempt to touch his skin. Instead of creating a connection, this unsuccessful act deepens her loss. Unable to take a breath, panic tightens her throat, and her racing heart wants to leap from her chest.

Only the surviving spouse is truly alone. Most people would be-lieve that the funeral is the worst part. But the funeral happened so fast, at a time when she was still numb and going through the mo-tions, in a state of shock and disbelief. In the following weeks, the void manifested, and she felt alone and lost. At first, it took a small foothold, then like a virus, it expanded rapidly, spreading into every imaginable cell in her body until she became the virus. That's when she became friends with self-pity. Brett's accident wasn't an isolated event that happened to him; it impacted her life as well. Now, after his death, she's the one left standing, needing to learn how to cope in the world alone. She recalls a recent nightmare from a week ago.

She was in an airport. When the announcement came to board the plane, she couldn't find Brett. She got out of line and started searching everywhere. Soon, all the passengers had boarded, and the door to the jetway was closing. Frantic after her search for him came up empty, her thoughts of abandonment were overwhelming. Awakened by her screams, Rita came running, thinking the worst.

Reliving that dream causes a renewed sense of abandonment. As her fears turn into anger, she grabs the hangers, and in a rage, she throws the clothes on the floor, heaping one armful after another onto the pile until the bar stands empty. Kneeling, she flings herself onto the pile and wails, distressed over her new fragility. How could he leave her? His clothing surrounds her like a bed of toxic flowers, and she's paralyzed, unwilling to go on. Life isn't fair.

Hours must have passed. She awakens to the sound of someone banging on the front door.

"Gabby, you in there?"

It is Carole.

Where did the day go? She stands up and runs her fingers through her disheveled hair, then opens the door.

"I've been knocking and ringing the bell for about five minutes. I was ready to call for help." Carole's intense expression and loud voice differ from her usual professional calmness.

"I must have fallen asleep."

Alarmed by Gabby's pale face and flat affect, Carole pushes past Gabby without waiting for an invitation. "I thought we were doing this together. How long have you been here?"

"A while—since morning. What time is it?"

"It's nearly 4:00 p.m. We had an appointment." Carole's heart fills with empathy as she steps around the glass on the floor. She picks up the broken frame and notes the photo of Gabby's wedding.

In a softer tone, she says, "Tell me about your day. I could use some water. I'll get you some too." She walks into the kitchen, turns on the faucet. Not a drop. Curious, she opens the refrigerator and finds it empty. "Gabby, the water's turned off. You've been here all day." She sets down her bag. "Good thing I brought sandwiches." She turns to Gabby and reaches for her hand. "I'm glad I'm here. Show me where to turn on the water. Then we'll eat and talk."

After turning on the water and dining on sandwiches, Carole asks Gabby for a tour of the house. Upon entering the rooms, Carol asks questions, getting Gabby to talk casually about her married life with Brett. Not once does she break down as she shares stories and the significance of some of the objet d'art. It's the most she's spoken since Brett was transferred to the hospital.

Carole turns the corner to the master bedroom and views the pile of clothing on the floor.

"Is this what you were doing today?"

Gabby nods.

"Care to tell me about it?"

Gabby hangs her head and bites her upper lip. "I was mad because he left me."

"It was an accident. He didn't plan to leave you."

"It was stupid. He would be here today if he hadn't gotten on the back of that bull."

"Nothing can change that. What you can change is how you go forward. Staying angry is your choice. Or you can choose to focus on your good memories, just like you did today as you showed me your house." Carole looks closely into her eyes. "You made some real progress today. Coming here took courage. I'm proud of you. However, it's been a long day, and we're both tired. I'll drop you off with your family on my way out." She reaches for the light switch. "Lean on your family. It will be easier if you do."

Gabby nods and looks around one more time as if trying to memorize the details before closing the door and locking it.

Carole drives down the lane and stops at the main house. She places her hand on Gabby's shoulder. "Your home is beautiful. Thanks for showing it to me."

Gabby reluctantly opens the car door. Can she get through the night without Carole's guidance?

"I'll see you at my office in two days."

Biting her lip, she softly says, "Goodnight."

CHAPTER 31

October

There are hints of yellow on the trees, and there's a crisp coolness in the morning air. Fall is arriving late this year. Gabby takes a sip of her coffee as she rocks on the front porch, listening to the ducks quack and watching them swim on the nearby lake. She moved back into her house two weeks after Carole's visit. She boxed up the large heap of Brett's clothing for the church's thrift store and chose to save a flannel work shirt that still carried his scent. She wears it to bed even though her belly makes it impossible to close the last button. She has it on now with a pair of sweatpants.

Yesterday was her last full day at the horse center, so she made a promise to watch the sunrise this morning. It was splendid and gave her hope that her future will be brighter. In her hand is a small wooden horse. Gregg, the older veteran from the horse center, carved it himself and proudly presented the gift on her last day of work. She was deeply touched, and whenever she sees it, she'll think of Brett, the horse center, and also of Gregg. She feels a common bond with the kind soul who has also suffered a loss.

Surprisingly, she's excited about the events taking place this evening. Her daddy is sponsoring a fundraising dinner for Richard's campaign. She hasn't seen Richard since that Sunday in her daddy's office. At times she misses him, which surprises her. Maybe it's the wacky hormones that make her nostalgic. The baby's been active and kicking all hours of the day and night. She'd like to share that with him. She wonders if he thinks about her or their child since he hasn't called.

She had a sonogram at her last appointment, but she chose not to learn the sex. After what happened with Jacob, she can't go through that again. Ella has been great, and she calls Gabby almost every day. They Zoom so she can see little Gracie, and she marvels at how fast she is growing. Gracie is sitting on her own and is trying to crawl. Will she be as good a mother as Ella seems to be? Ella's Will is a wonderful father, and it saddens her to think that her baby will grow up without a father.

But her daddy set the rules that she and Richard are to follow. At the time, she agreed that it was best, but lately, she feels differently and would like to share. Her daddy said they couldn't be seen in public together, and Richard hasn't made any attempts to see her or ask about her pregnancy.

At the dinner tonight, Richard will make the official announcement that he is entering the gubernatorial race. All eyes will be on him, including hers. This will be her first public appearance as a pregnant widow. For the occasion, she ordered a dress from a maternity catalog, and she has rehearsed her line that conveys the agreed-upon story, the father of the baby is her former husband.

Stan and Marie have offered to drive her into the city, but she declined because she wants to check out her condo, do some shopping, and have a long overdue hair appointment.

Later that evening, standing inside the hotel's lobby before the dinner, she waits for her daddy and Rita. A man with a journalist badge walks quickly toward her from the far side, so she turns away.

"Ms. King," he shouts as if it's urgent.

"Yes?"

"Hunter, with the *City News.* I have a few questions."

"Yes."

"Can you define your relationship with Senator Wright?"

She smiles to cover her uneasiness and hesitates. "He's a family friend."

"Rumor has it around town that you are more than friends. In fact, there is talk that he is the father of your…"

"Excuse me." She turns away from him and reaches out to her daddy as he and Rita arrive.

"Hi, Daddy." She kisses him on the cheek, which always brings a smile. "Rita." She reaches out for her hand. "You both look rather dashing."

She turns back to the journalist. "This is my daddy, Wayne King, and, I'm sorry, what is your name again? I'm sure Daddy will be happy to answer all of your questions about Senator Wright."

She moves away and pulls Rita along.

"Thanks for saving me." Her heart pounds.

Rita's forehead creases. "Care to share?"

"A reporter looking for a story." She casts her eyes downward.

"Wayne will take care of him. I'm sorry." Rita senses Gabby's fearfulness and squeezes her hand. "I love your hair and that green dress," she says. "I'm excited for tonight. It's been a while since we've had a proper night out."

King rejoins them. "Offensive man, isn't he? He won't be bothering you again. I threatened to get his ass fired." He searches the lobby as if looking for another adversary. "Excuse me, ladies. I need to take care of some last-minute details. I'll see you in the ballroom." He bows and then heads off.

"Always working, that man," Rita says, watching King as he walks to a group of men.

She scans the lobby as more people arrive. "He's been working on Richard's bid for governor for five years. This next year will be the most important, right up to election night. We've come too far to have some meddlesome reporter spreading rumors." Rita holds out her arm. "Let's see that grand ballroom, shall we?"

As anticipated, the room is decorated in red, white, and blue, with huge stars hanging from the ceiling above the podium. Two large sprays of flowers grace the stage on both sides, and the tables sport smaller versions of the same. The room is set for about three hundred guests.

"Gabby, it's so wonderful to see you again," a deep voice says, getting closer.

She turns to see Steven Prime walking toward her. "A sight for my eyes, two stunning ladies. King sure is a lucky man."

"Mr. Prime, it's so nice to see you again. You've met my stepmother, Rita."

"Please, Gabby, Rita, call me Steve. I would rather dine with you lovely creatures, but I have a table with some fledgling IT entrepreneurs."

She smiles. "They'll be honored to be at your table."

"There's a reason why I like you. You seem to know what to say to make an old man feel young again." A commotion at the doorway drowns out his chuckle.

In the center of the crowd is Richard. She bites her inner cheek and rolls her shoulders back. As always, he looks impeccable, every hair in place. He is dressed in a black tux. Part of her feels special thinking that she could have him, and the other part of her feels guilty that she has any feelings for him since her husband has been gone only a few months.

"He seems to have gotten your attention, along with a dozen others," Prime remarks.

She feels the heat rush to her face.

"He has a charisma about him, reminds me of that Clinton fellow. He owns the room—everyone's aware he's there. He'll make a great governor. Ladies." He leaves them.

She wipes her tear before it falls down her cheek. "I'm sorry."

"It must be hard for you. I can't imagine." Rita reaches for her hand.

"I'm being silly. It must be the hormones."

Rita hands her a tissue. "It's the night of his life."

"I'm happy for him. I'm a bit surprised that he's alone."

"Wayne says that Richard and Amanda have been pretty tight. I thought you should know." Rita stretches to look around the crowd. "She's there, in the back. She just came through the door."

In a red dress that looks like it came off a Paris runway, Amanda exudes confidence. Her six-inch heels and the long slit up the side of the dress make her shapely legs look as though they go on a mile. If every woman in the room is enthralled with Richard, Amanda will have captivated every red-blooded male. Her long dark hair shines under the lights and makes a cape over her shoulders.

"Wow, she certainly is stunning," Rita says.

Gabby watches as Richard turns and takes Amanda's hand. She sees their genuine smiles, and it's as if someone has punched her in the gut as the realization hits her: they are America's perfect couple. They will appear on every state magazine cover. Gabby might be carrying his child, but the press and the citizens of Texas will see Richard, the candidate for governor, with Amanda by his side. Looking away doesn't ease the pain because the image of them together is etched in her mind.

However, this is the necessary plan to meet the goal that both she and Richard agreed upon. Why is her ego so fragile? Is it because Richard hasn't arranged to see her or even phone her? Is it because his relationship with Amanda comes across as real? Is it?

The guests take their chairs, and the State Attorney General gives the welcome. A banker and his wife are seated at King's table, along with Stan and Marie. Introductions are made all around, which briefly provides Gabby a distraction; however, the position of her chair forces her to face Richard and Amanda every time she lifts her eyes from her plate.

Needing a different view midway through the meal, she offers an excuse and leaves the ballroom. Down the hallway, double doors lead to the courtyard, a place to find refuge.

Upon her return, she finds Richard seated in the hall, scrolling through his phone. Deep in concentration, he doesn't hear her heels clicking on the tiled floor. She takes a deep breath and approaches.

"Tonight is big. You look great."

"Gabby, yes, thanks." He doesn't look up. "I'm reviewing the names of our biggest donors. Amanda usually reminds me. She's great at putting names to faces."

"She seems to enjoy the attention."

He continues scrolling as if searching for something in particular. "Amanda loves this life. Whenever I complain, she's quick to tell me again that it's the people that matter."

"Are you sleeping with her?" The words are fast from her mind to her lips, and she can't take them back.

He looks up with wide eyes. "Why would you care? I didn't hear any complaints from you about King's plan. I remember being the only one objecting."

She lowers her eyes.

"Yes, I'm sleeping with her. It's easy, unlike us, and we're together all the time." He looks like a little boy daring to be punished when caught with his hand in the cookie jar but continues to grab the delicious treats.

She's silent as her mind struggles to grip the painful words. They cut through her like a sword.

"Gabby, you pushed me away months ago. You have no grounds to complain."

"I'm carrying your child."

"A child that I can't be a father to. Think about that. You agreed that it would be political suicide." He stands and shakes his head. "We're not supposed to be seen together, remember? I'm sorry if this upsets you. Sometimes life sucks, so deal with it. I have to get back inside."

She watches him disappear, and full of rage, her body shakes. She's angry because he's been avoiding her, and she feels neglected. However, he is pinning the reason for his absence on her and is avoiding all responsibility. He neglected to ask how she feels, and he didn't even compliment her looks. Her hand covers her stomach, and as she compares her pregnant body to Amanda's shapely physique, she shudders. Her insecurities are mounting.

Sadness and disappointment threaten to overwhelm her since her expectations of finally seeing Richard and having some time together have been different from reality. It's as if he doesn't care. But what did she expect? Did she think he would put his love life on hold for a year so he could run for governor and she could have the baby? It is a tough mess, one that will leave her a single mother. God, she wants to hate every selfish bone in his body.

Hearing a round of loud applause, she hurries back to the ballroom where King has taken the podium, ready to introduce Richard. Gabby glances at Amanda and sees the gorgeous brunette sitting forward in her seat, her face beaming as she watches Richard. *Maybe they do belong together.*

"Welcome, welcome. How was dinner?" Richard pauses for the applause. "It has been quite a journey fighting for the rights of the people of this great state. I helped bring down a drug lord to stop the drugs from coming over our border, and I put a halt to human trafficking." He pauses as a round of applause breaks out, nodding in acknowledgment of the audience's praise. "But there are even bigger goals that we're capable of accomplishing together. Let's make our state the greatest for new technologies, the best economy, the most jobs for our citizens. Let's promote better education and increase services. Who is with me?"

Cheers fill the room. Everyone is on their feet, and the smile on

Richard's face grows wide. He's radiating a contagious positivity that has the entire room spellbound. He emits a desire that Gabby has never witnessed, and as his passion mesmerizes the crowd, at this moment, she is sure they would do anything for him.

"Tonight, I make my bid to run for governor of the great state of Texas."

Music fills the room. The confetti and balloons fall from nets attached to the ceiling. King stands close, and Richard motions for Amanda to join them on stage.

The brunette takes the stairs and turns to wave to the crowd before joining Richard. The cheers get louder, and Amanda pulls Richard close for a kiss. At this moment, Gabby is sure that she has lost Richard. He will never be a father to his child.

Filled with extreme sadness, she's all alone amid hundreds. She bites her upper lip as emptiness gnaws her stomach. Immediately, a warmth radiates as she feels a hand on her back. Stan always has a way of reading her thoughts. She doesn't dare meet his eyes because she will be unable to handle the tears that are certain to flow. Very gently, she leans into him, and his hand moves to her waist. It seems as though he understands.

CHAPTER 32

That night after the campaign rally is over and the crowd has dispersed, Gabby arrives alone at her downtown condo. She purchased the condo years ago after returning from New York to market her art and held on to it for its convenience to downtown. This will be her first night within the four walls since Brett died.

After closing the front door, she shuts the world out. She's safe. Here, there will be no surprises to prompt emotional meltdowns. Tonight at the campaign dinner, in hopes of preserving her sanity, she had wished to escape early. That was impossible because she was expected to support the campaign. Her daddy frequently stresses the importance of family and paraphrases a verse from the Bible, "If you can't manage your own family, you can't manage others."

Tonight, it became as clear as a hard slap to her face that going forward, Richard will most likely not be part of her future family. This hurts more than she thought it would. In the past, she was the one who dictated the terms of their relationship: the called-off engagement, then marrying Brett. And recently, she's the one who demanded distance by ignoring his phone calls and texts. She only has herself to blame for practically throwing him into Amanda's arms. But does she deserve to play the role of the victim?

She must look pathetic to an outsider—a recent widow who was unfaithful to her dying husband, crying over a lost relationship that she pretended she didn't want. The situation leaves her craving a drink. But she can't drown her sorrows with alcohol, and she wonders if this is the same logical reasoning that makes her desire Richard's attention. Does the thought of not having him and seeing him happy with Amanda cause her to want him that much more? That's pretty sick, something she will bring up with Carole at her next therapy session.

Turning her thoughts to Stan lightens her mood. Without any words said between them, she's sure he identifies with her feelings. It's almost as if she and Stan are from the same blood. Tonight, he was there at one of her lowest times, and she's aware that if she called him any time of the day or night, he would be by her side. He was there for her during her pregnancy with Jacob, and she recalls his hurt when she chose Brett. Now she's beginning to understand how he must have felt. At that time, the level of his hurt hadn't occurred to her. Now in a similar situation, she has more empathy.

As she turns over in bed to read the clock, she sees that it's 1:00 a.m., and she's still wide awake. She throws off the covers and sits up straight before sliding her feet to the floor, remembering an article that said if you have trouble sleeping, it's better to get out of the bed and do something productive than to toss and turn for hours.

The fundraiser was unsettling, and the image of Amanda and Richard flashes in her mind, even with her eyes closed.

After getting a glass of milk, she retrieves her art supplies from the closet. It will be the first time that she's tried to paint since Brett's passing.

Her canvas measures three feet on the vertical axis and four feet on the horizontal as she sets it on the easel in landscape orientation. Squeezing the paint from the tubes onto her palette is one of her favorite tasks. The paint smells fresh, and the small piles of the gooey substance make a rainbow of vibrant colors.

Unable to rid her mind of the fundraiser, she fills her brush full of blue paint for the background, similar to the shade of blue of the banners announcing, "Richard Wright is the Right Choice for Governor." Continuing with the color scheme, next, she applies a vibrant red, brushing the paint so that it almost divides the canvas in half. With a background of red on the top and blue on the bottom, she adds obscure white images in varying sizes that could read as far-away stars to a viewer.

At a quick glance, her canvas reminds her of the famous artist Jasper Johns, who is known for his flags. She loves the Texas flag and what it represents: the open flat land, ranches, longhorn cattle, oil derricks, cowboy hats and boots. She respects the history, that Texas was its own country for ten years and fought for its independence from Mexico. The people here are proud, hardworking folks, and deals are frequently made over an honest handshake. She also loves that Texas is known for the live music scene. Many musicians get their start playing in the numerous local bars. Thinking about Texas makes her happy. She cranks up the music on her phone. This painting may not be a masterpiece, but it's worth a million bucks for her mental lift.

Her daddy has worked for many years to position Richard for the announcement he made tonight, and she would be acting like a spoiled brat if she did anything going forward to compromise his efforts.

Painting this representational image of the flag moves her to consider the idea of freedom. She has the freedom to step back, to observe her situation from an outsider's perspective. She has the freedom to enjoy her pregnancy, find herself, evaluate her future, and then set the goals necessary to get to where she wants to be. She doesn't need a man by her side to accomplish these ends. Why is she giving Richard her power and allowing him to steal her peace?

One question begs an answer: Who is she now that she's single again? Besides her current state of fragility and floundering, the answer to this important question will help determine her future. She's in a vulnerable period of transition.

She's never been on her own because there have always been men lined up, eager to be by her side. Now, a widow and with Richard in another relationship, she's in uncharted territory. She wonders about silly things like, is she grieving properly? Should she have been in black tonight instead of the emerald green that matched Brett's eyes?

Weeks ago, after the baptism of little Gracie, Stan questioned the proper etiquette for being a godparent. She jokingly suggested that he use Google to find a book on the subject. Maybe she should take her own advice and Google how to be the proper widow. However, she doubts she'll find etiquette for her dilemma. She ponders why many women define themselves by the man standing at their side. Before she invites anyone into her circle, she needs to heal from Brett's death and discover who she is. She needs to blaze her path, a path for her and her child.

Richard can choose to be involved in their child's life or not. She can't control that. Why is she going down the self-pity road and giving away the power to determine her happiness? It all seems pretty ludicrous. To hell with Richard. She's taking control.

Stepping away from her canvas, she observes that creating this painting has given her clarity, and the energy has given in to natural tiredness. She yawns, ready to hit the sack for some blessed sleep.

CHAPTER 33

ArtSmart Gallery

Opening the door to Rita's gallery, the familiar tingling of the bells brings comfort.

"Good morning, Gabby." Rita sees Gabby struggling with her artist travel bag in one hand and the large canvas in her other and rushes to assist. "What do you have here?"

"It's a canvas that I'm going to paint over." She sets the canvas against the counter and wipes her brow. "I should hit the gym. I'll never be able to push this baby out in my current state of fitness."

"You've got time. Check with your doctor first, okay?" She studies the painting. "When did you do this? It's not your usual style."

"You're right. I was fooling around last night after the fundraiser."

Rita has her hand on her chin as though in deliberation. "Did I hear you say that you were going to paint over this?"

"Yes, like you were quick to point out, it's not my style."

"It reminds me of a Jasper Johns."

197

"I thought the same."

"Jasper was known to put numbers and random letters in most of his works."

"Funny you should say that because I wanted to write *freedom* in big letters."

Rita continues staring at the canvas. "I can see it."

"Keep going...you can see what?" Rita's got her interest.

"Scrawl the word *freedom* on it, like graffiti on a city wall. Then apply some thick paint in strategic places in a dry-brush style, giving it some grit since freedom comes with a struggle, and to finish, add a few washes to give it depth, and then it could be perfect." She nods her head in approval. "I can sell that. What do you think?"

"I can do that. It seems a little silly, but, Rita, I've learned to trust your judgment."

"Great, I can't wait to put it on the wall. I have just the place. Are you going to work on it today?"

"If that's all right."

"Look around. No customers. Instead of working in the back, set up here. Clients love to see an artist at work."

Gabby looks around the gallery. "Where is everyone?"

"The girls have been working every day when I was at the ranch, you know, helping with you." She looks down at her feet, then clasps her hands together. "Anyway, since I was in town for Richard's announcement, I gave the girls a much-deserved day off. The gallery has been doing well. We sold more last month than in the previous six months combined. Check out your wall. I had to use other artist's works to fill in the spaces."

"Great, it'll be you and me, just like the good ole days." She smiles.

"In that case, while you set up over in the corner, I'm going to make us some tea. We had some good times here. Let's make some more memories."

Gabby bites her upper lip. Yes, she has had some good times here, and many of those included Brett. He was known for his antics when he met her at the studio.

Closing her eyes, she remembers:

She was working on a Saturday afternoon an hour before closing time. As she was ringing up a customer's purchase, the bells jingled. Assuming another client was coming to browse, she didn't give it another thought. When she heard his voice ushering the man with his purchase out after bidding him a good day, she heard the click of the lock.

Rita had lectured her just an hour ago about failing to keep the gallery open until the posted closing time. It seems that the previous Saturday, one of her buyers arrived during regular business hours, and the closed sign was displayed.

Today, Brett had that big grin on his face, the one that made his dimple deeper. He then proceeded to turn off the lights.

"I have another hour. You can relax in the back. Get a beer out of the fridge." She tried her best to sound like she had authority, determined that he wasn't going to get his way.

"You're right, I'm going in the back, but you, the hard-working, gorgeous artist are going back there with me. I'll rub your feet, and what happens next will depend on your sales pitch."

"Brett, I can't. But it's an incredible offer. Raincheck in an hour?"

"Tell me your total sales today, and I'll match it. Best deal you made today." He backs her against a wall and reaches up her skirt.

"We could have had a remarkable day. Best day of the year."

"But you didn't," he whispers in her ear and then lifts her blouse to

caress her breast. "I've been casing the place, and the guy who just left has been your only customer since lunch."

"You're bluffing."

"You're denying it? Show me proof."

"You're so bad. Rita will be mad."

"Rita will never know." He lifts her off her feet and carries her into the back room. "Let her fire you."

Her eyes are closed, and she's smiling. Brett always got his way. He'd put on the charm, and she'd be mesmerized. Other people told her that time had a way of healing. She didn't believe it, but she's still standing after revisiting this memory, and the mascara's not running black down her cheeks. Is she getting accustomed to the emptiness his void has caused?

She sets up her easel and dons an apron, then gets to work. Using pressure on the flat brush, she writes the word *freedom* to make a statement of importance. The letters are scrawled in blood red and painted imperfectly to illustrate struggle. Then she applies thick paint in the dry-brush method, which leaves bits of the background showing underneath and gives a rustic feel to the composition. Finishing as Rita suggested, she does several pale washes in shades of gray, making sure that each layer is dry before applying the next.

Caught up in her work, she's unaware of the presence looking over her shoulder.

"Gabby," a male voice says.

Startled, she jumps.

Richard is grinning. "It's nice to know that I still have that effect on you."

Her face is turning red, and she wipes the brush on her cloth before putting it in the water container.

"Don't flatter yourself. It could have been a homeless man or a bent-over old maid."

He chuckles. "There's energy in this painting. I feel honored that I inspire you."

She stands and wipes her hands on her apron. It's awkward, having him standing over her, critiquing her work, and making it all about him.

"How is that...that you are the inspiration?"

"The colors are my colors."

"They are the colors of Texas."

"I used the word *freedom* in my speech last night."

"Freedom is a general term, used by many."

"As an artist, aren't you supposed to allow the viewer to interpret? Making the art personal to them sells more art."

"I was trying to get you to go deeper." She's saving herself and thinking fast. "As an artist, I want the viewer to go beneath the surface of what's visual. I want to reach his soul."

"Well said, good recovery." He laughs. "Gabriella, you never cease to amaze me."

She hasn't fooled him in the least. *Damn.*

"I'll make you a deal. Come to lunch, and I'll buy this masterpiece of yours and use it for my campaign. Imagine your work being seen on television, posters, billboards, and pamphlets all over Texas. Awesome, right?"

"I can't go to lunch with you. Remember the rules?"

"We can't be seen alone together, and we won't be. I'm meeting Amanda. She's my campaign manager." He dials his phone. "Hey, Amanda, walk down to the art gallery. I want to show you something...Great." He disconnects. "She's on her way."

She runs her fingers through her hair. She must look like a mess. *The perfect Amanda is coming here, now. Lord, help me.* Her baby kicks. "Oh," she says as she holds her stomach.

"Are you all right?" There is a wrinkle in his brow.

"The baby just kicked. It took me by surprise."

"Oh, okay. Hey, here's Amanda...love that gal, always on time and with a smile."

She rolls her eyes.

The gallery door opens, and Amanda looks near perfect, just like Gabby envisioned. Her long brunette hair is slightly out of place because of the breeze. Her blue suit fits impeccably—it must be designer—and her four-inch heels are the same color. She carries a red LV bag.

"Hey, what's up?" She takes his hand and nods to Gabby. "Gabriella, it's so nice to see you again."

Richard points to the canvas. "What do you think?"

"For our condo?"

"No, silly, for the campaign—our new look going forward now that the announcement has been made. You know, for posters and whatever."

"Let me see." Amanda puts her finger to her lips as if thinking and walks around to the opposite side. "Yes, this will work—if you like it. I'll need to develop a tagline that incorporates the word *freedom.* That's easy."

Richard smiles. "There, it's a done deal. It's perfect. Wrap it up while we're at lunch, and we can pick it up on our way back."

"It's still a bit wet, but in the hour, it should be dry."

"Get that apron off, and let's go. My treat."

"That's really sweet of you, but I can't. Some other time." She does her best to look disappointed.

"Suit yourself. I told Amanda that the Chinese food here is the best in town. We'll be back for the painting."

Amanda looks up to him and smiles with her pouty red lips. Gabby thinks she looks like a Barbie doll. *Did he say Chinese? That's her favorite. Does he have to share that with Amanda?*

They turn toward the door and then exit. Gabby wasn't aware that she had been holding her breath. She mulls over their conversation. Not once did he inquire about the baby. After she explained the baby's kick, she thought he should have asked something. Then later, did she hear him say that he loved Amanda, and did she say for "our condo?" Are they living together? *Wow, she didn't expect all of this news.*

The timing of their visit was terrible. Here she is looking like a frumpy housewife. She questions why she cares what Amanda thinks. *Face it, Gabby, you're jealous.* She doesn't want Richard, but she doesn't want Amanda to have him either.

Last night, she had come to a resolution to this problem. Didn't she decide to discover who she is and where she wants to go? She had chosen freedom to control her destiny. Was all of that just idle talk?

Rita comes over. "Hey, what was that all about?"

"It was Richard and Amanda. They bought the painting."

"You mean I don't get to put it on the wall? Let me see it."

"Wow, looks great. Make another."

"I did it just the way you described." She takes off her apron and folds it.

"But do you like it—you, as the artist?"

"It's growing on me but may take some time. They're coming back after lunch to pick it up."

"What price?"

"Rita, whatever you think. It's your store. You decide."

"Gabby, you okay? You're acting a little strange." She stands with hands on her hips as if waiting for an answer. "It must be hard seeing them together like that. I thought that maybe you and Richard would have a future together with the baby and all."

She waves her hands in the air, then rubs her forehead. "It's okay. I don't want to talk about it." She continues packing up her art supplies. "I'm going home. I'm tired."

"Sure thing, honey. Call if you want to talk. I'm here for you, okay?"

Gabby looks up with watery eyes. "I know. I love you for that."

CHAPTER 34

November

Gabby is at home trying to replace a burned-out light bulb. She crawls up on the kitchen island but still cannot reach the ceiling light. After stretching, she grabs her stomach with one hand and the small of her back with the other. She glances at her watch. It's early, just after seven o'clock in the evening. Remembering Stan's words, she dials his cell.

"Hey, sis." His voice is cheery.

"What are you doing?"

"Gabby, I know that tone. What do you need?"

"A lightbulb replaced."

"On my way."

"You sure Marie won't mind?"

"No, she's in the tub. That girl loves her bubble baths. Be there in five." There's a click.

She opens the garage door to get the ladder and starts to drag it around to the front door.

"Hey, stop. You shouldn't be doing that. I must not have gotten here fast enough. Maybe I should wear my boots when I'm at home. I'd get here faster." He grins. Ryder is at his side.

His smiling face always lifts her mood. She leans on the ladder. "I was trying to be helpful."

"Don't steal my thunder." He takes the ladder from her, and they walk together to the front door. "I'm glad you called. If I would have found out you were up on this ladder…" He shakes his head side-to-side. "A woman in your condition should not be on a ladder. You should call more often."

"Okay. I'll call you when I need these gutters cleaned. The leaves are dropping fast this year."

His eyes meet hers. "How are you doing?"

"Good." She turns away from him and pets Ryder. "You're a good dog. Want a treat?"

"Gabby, this is me. Changing the subject isn't going to work. Let's try again. How are you really doing? Something is bothering you."

"You read me too well." She goes into the pantry for the dog treat.

"It's because I care. Someone needs to look after you, now that Brett's… Geez, I'm sorry, I sure stuck my foot in my mouth." He looks around her foyer. "Where's this light?"

"In the kitchen. I thought I could stand on the counter."

"Whoa there, lady. I'm better off not knowing." He points his thumbs into his chest. "Stan, your handyman, is here now. You could see Ryder more often if you would let me do more for you." She does miss spending time with Ryder. Maybe she should get a dog.

206

He climbs up the ladder and hands her the burned-out bulb. Screwing in the new one, he asks again, "So what's bothering you?"

"It's Richard."

"What else is new? I've heard that from you before."

"He doesn't seem interested in the baby."

"If I understand the situation, he's forbidden."

"He doesn't even ask. And then there is Amanda." She pauses. "He's sleeping with her."

"Not a surprise. They looked pretty tight at the fundraiser. She's a ten."

"Great, thanks. It's wonderful to know that you think so too." She looks down at her belly.

"You're feeling insecure. Gabby, you're a ten, but in a different way. You're beautiful and classy. Amanda, she's... umm, she's ambitious and has a suggestive air about her. Yeah, that's a good way to describe it." He starts to climb down the ladder.

"You and every other male in the room were drooling."

"She and Richard seem to be from the same mold. They look good together. You're not jealous, are you?" He flips on the switch, and the light shines bright.

"No...maybe. I thought he cared after we slept together."

"Honest, Gabby, how did that happen? I'd like to understand."

"I don't know. It was a big mistake. I was lonely. I was tired. It just happened."

"Like I said, you should have called me."

"I didn't call Richard. He showed up with wine and Chinese food and...whatever."

"And whatever...sex for you is whatever."

She takes notice of his harsh tone. "Don't you judge me. You don't know what it was like—day in and day out, watching him suffer."

"I would have been there for you. You didn't give me a chance." He throws his hands up in the air, picks up the ladder, and heads for the front door. Ryder follows.

She runs after him. His disapproval weighs heavy on her heart. "I'm sorry, Stan. I'm so sorry. It's a mess."

"Nothing new. This seems to be your norm." He closes the garage door after putting the ladder away. "I'm sorry too."

Sadness seems to wash over him, and he turns his back.

"Goodnight." He hangs his head and walks down the lane toward his house. His limp is more noticeable.

"Back so soon?" Marie calls from the bedroom after Stan opens the front door.

She's in her black lace nightgown, her long brunette tresses still damp from her bath.

"She needed a lightbulb changed in her kitchen. It didn't take much." He sits down on the armchair in the great room. "I'm glad she called because she tried to change it by standing on the kitchen counter."

She comes to sit on his lap. "She shouldn't do that."

"I told her the same thing."

"She rubs his neck and kisses him on the cheek. "You're a good man, Stan." She stands and pulls on his arm. "Come to bed."

"You go on. I'll be there in a few minutes."

Stan scratches his head, then stands and looks out his kitchen window at Gabby's house. He beholds the night sky. It was Gabby who taught him to appreciate the universe and encouraged him to wish on stars. The evening star shines the brightest, but each star begs to be his chosen recipient. However, he sends no wishes and turns away.

"Crazy woman… or am I a crazy man?" he mutters under his breath before switching off the light.

CHAPTER 35

The holiday season came fast. Thanksgiving had the whole King family together. King likes nothing better than to be surrounded by family at the dining room table. He always has stories to tell and sometimes laughs heartily before delivering a punchline. He invited Richard, but Amanda was taking him to meet her family in Houston.

When she heard the news of Richard's absence, Gabby's initial irritation gave way to proper thinking and led to relief because she didn't want to ruin Thanksgiving for the family. She's angry with Richard for neglecting her and his child. Not once has he called to inquire as to her well-being. If standing face-to-face, her rage would lead to an attack. She understands from conversations with her father that the campaign trail depletes his time and energy, but that doesn't excuse Richard from not phoning.

She was willing to work something out for the sake of their child, but since months have gone by with silence, he's proving himself to be undeserving. Richard takes on the likes of a traitor because he led her to believe that he had changed. She was under the impression that he wanted this pregnancy. Is she wrong? Ultimately, the role he decides to play in their child's life is his choice.

Was she so desperate the evening he came over last spring that she also misread his intentions? His tender lovemaking gave her reason to think he loved her. However, who is she to judge? She didn't love him then and probably still doesn't today. Since Amanda is introducing him to her family, their relationship must be serious. It baffles her that her calmness gives way to agitation whenever she thinks about him, and that seems to be more times than she would like to admit.

CHAPTER 36

December

These past two months, Gabby has vowed to put herself first. After quitting work at the Equine-Assisted Therapy Center, she's had time to paint, read, hike around the ranch, rock on her porch, sit on the dock at the lake, and think about Brett and the baby. During these activities, she has caught herself twirling her hair so often that she began to notice loose strands wrapped around her fingers and a bald spot appearing above her ear. Since then, she's more aware, and now instead of reaching for a strand of hair, her fingernails take the brunt of her nervous anxiety. Her meditation practice needs work.

When she thinks of Brett, she wonders if he sees her and knows of her struggles. During those first months after he was gone, she prayed to feel his presence because she read that other people have had those experiences. She tried hard to see him in the birds chirping overhead, in the wildflowers spreading over the fields, or possibly a message in the buzz of a honeybee. Then, she thought maybe he was trying to get her attention at night when she awakened to a creak or a bump. *Is that Brett?* But she feels no connection, only fear.

As time creeps forward without any signs affirming his presence, she struggles to prevent her descent down the dark staircase of loneliness and guilt. Is she unable to feel his presence because he's angry? God has forgiven her, so Brett has forgiven her, right? She talks through these negative moments by replacing them with positive thoughts in an effort to flood light into the deluge of pessimistic thinking. Carole reassures her during her weekly visits that she's making progress. Sometimes, she has doubts.

With the baby due in three months, she has painted the nursery a light gray. In a nesting mood, she has been crocheting, a craft her grandmother passed to her, and has made two blankets and a pair of booties. She's also painted—one canvas has two little bears in pink tutus, a gift for Ella to hang in little Gracie's room, and a second for her own nursery, with one bear in a pink tutu and the other bear in a blue suit. It brings her joy to find it in the nursery, along with the crib and the rocking chair.

She called Stan when the crib was delivered, and as he assembled it, he shared some vignettes of his life growing up with his brother. She sat in the rocking chair and felt sorry for Will as the man assembling the crib boasted about the horrible pranks he played on his little brother. She wonders if her baby will ever have a sibling.

To prepare for the delivery, she's been watching online birthing classes. A dull sadness looms over her, knowing that she'll bring this child into the world on her own. Maybe she'll ask Jamie to help with the birth since Jamie has been like a mother to her. She's also been working on her fitness for an easier birth, developing and strengthening her core muscles by practicing yoga with a prenatal yoga DVD.

Becoming aware that in a matter of weeks, she'll be unable to reach down and tie her shoes prompts her to order some slip-on shoes a size larger than she usually wears to compensate for her swollen feet and ankles. She's doing all she can to be ready.

With the arrival of the winter months, she's been calling Stan regularly for odd jobs around the house, and he's always helpful, but she remembers that he used to smile more. When asked, he reports that he and Marie are fine. She misses working with him at the horse center.

While she nestles under her blanket, gazing at a roaring fire in her family room, large white flurries dance in the air outside. Snow in Texas is rare and, in December, priceless. The falling snow reminds her of the fast-approaching holiday. She's decided not to decorate for Christmas because it seems like too much work, and taking it down at a time nearer to her due date would make it that much more la-bor-intensive.

Closing her eyes, she thinks of Brett and the wonderful life they shared. Time does have a way of making it hurt less, but the hole is still there, though it doesn't threaten to suck her into its vortex like it once did. She loved him and always will, and she believes that his love for her was equally as strong. This gives her comfort.

She holds her stomach. Over these past months, she has been more peaceful and feels blessed to have a fresh start with the life grow-ing inside her. God has given her this gift to keep her afloat through the dark periods, and now, what she once thought was a curse is a true blessing. Her daddy always wanted a grandchild, and his eyes twinkle whenever they discuss the baby. He's a rock, his wisdom valuable, so to please him, she legally changed her name back to King. She'll tell him on Christmas Day.

Three days before Christmas, there's a knock at her door. She's not expecting anyone. As she peers out the window, she sees Stan. *I wonder what he wants.*

"Hey, Stan," she says, opening the door. "Are you out walking in the snow?"

"Hi! Merry Christmas!" He wears a big grin and holds a six-foot pine. "I brought you a Christmas tree. You going to stand there or invite me in?"

"Oh yes, sorry." She opens the door wide for him to come through.

"Where do you want this?"

She holds her chin, thinking deeply before answering. "Over here by the window would be nice. You'll be able to see the lights from your house, and it's away from the fire."

"Good choice."

He sets rocks around the base to secure the tree, then puts water in the bucket. "Be right back."

Her brow is furrowed. She mops up the wet trail of residue from his snow-covered boots. Stan returns with a box.

"What's in there?"

"Decorations, of course. A tree isn't a Christmas tree unless it has decorations. While I untangle these lights, why don't you put on some Christmas music and make us some hot cocoa? I see you already have the fire. Good, because baby, it's cold outside." He starts to sing the familiar holiday tune.

"When I was here the other day, I didn't see one sign of Christmas. I love Christmas. I thought you did too." He unwinds an extension cord and plugs it into the outlet before starting to empty the contents of the cardboard box on her coffee table.

Returning from the kitchen with a tray holding two mugs of hot cocoa and a plate of cookies, she watches as he adds the strings of lights. It's a thoughtful gesture, but that's Stan.

"Marie didn't want to come?"

"Marie left this morning for San Diego. She wants to spend Christmas with her family, and then she'll be back to celebrate New Year's Eve."

"Yes, sorry, I forgot." She looks at the boxes of ornaments. "These are so cute." She holds up miniature glass horses with wreaths of green around their necks. In the box, there are also horseshoe ornaments and little saddles.

"I saw those online. They were your Christmas gift. Since I'm using them now, I had to buy you another gift."

"You didn't have to."

"Gabby, I want to. I know it's hard. No one should have to face everything you did this year and now be all alone. I had to do something. You're my best friend. Hey, I've been thinking about those Lamaze classes. I can be your partner."

"That may be a bit weird, don't you think?" She crosses her arms.

"I won't look below the waist. Promise. I can't stand the sight of blood. I'll hold your hand and help you breathe or pant or whatever. I can do that."

"Again, I need to ask, what about Marie? Would she be okay with all of this?"

"I haven't asked, but why not? She knows we're friends. Heck, we're better than friends; we're family." He laughs out loud. "Think about it."

She hears him humming to the tunes on the radio. "Hey, I'm not decorating this by myself. Get over here."

"Yes, of course. Thanks, Stan. This is very thoughtful of you." She takes one of the saddle ornaments over to the tree.

"It's nice to see you smile." He turns when she blushes.

After the decorations are up, they sit on the couch to admire their work.

"It really is lovely. I have been missing Christmas." She leans into his arm.

He moves to pull her in closer. "It is lovely. And it's snowing. That's magical."

"Thanks for everything you've done for me lately. I know I haven't always been…pleasant."

"You've been fine. It's understandable. I made the right decision in selling my condo in Washington."

"You made that decision because of me?" She doesn't dare look at his face.

"Not entirely. But you were a big part of it."

She wasn't aware that she was holding her breath.

"I love the ranch, the horses, and the work at the center. And when Brett had his accident, it just confirmed that I made the right choice."

"I'm happy you stayed here in Texas." She pats his knee.

"Me too."

The awkward silence is broken by "Jingle Bells." Stan, in a baritone voice, belts out the tune, and she laughs. *Everything is going to be all right, just like Daddy told her months before.*

CHAPTER 37

Christmas Eve

Christmas Eve in a bustling Texas city is enchanting: the colored lights, the musicians on street corners bellowing familiar tunes, and the massive crowds filling the streets barricaded from automobiles to allow generous walking space for the patrons. There is a chill in the air. A church, whose congregation includes heavy donors, has asked Richard to give the opening remarks at their city hall Christmas Eve ceremony. The event is late afternoon, giving the King family plenty of time afterward to drive the two hours back to the ranch for their own celebration.

Gabby and Rita start the day at the gallery, giving the regular employees a holiday party, followed by a surprise announcement of a week off since Rita will keep the gallery closed until after New Year's.

As they gather the empty champagne flutes, Rita says, "It's so nice to close the year on a positive note. I appreciate our girls, and this year, the gallery is in the black."

"You're so good to them…and to me. I don't know how I would have gotten through this year without you and Jamie. Thank you." She hugs Rita, followed by a kiss on the cheek.

"We're family, and that's what family is all about." She turns, her tone serious. "I hear you've been spending a lot of time with Stan."

"It was sweet of him to bring over the tree and help me decorate. You raised a very thoughtful man."

Rita continues cleaning up the gallery. "I'm happy that he and Marie are together."

"Me too."

Rita smiles. "I'm glad to hear you say that. He's a sensitive and caring soul, and I would hate for him to get hurt."

Gabby lowers her eyes, uneasy with Rita's implication. She chooses to let it pass without comment.

The crowd size isn't what King had hoped it would be. However, the camera crew with ties to a major television station makes up for it. Over a million people will view Richard on the five o'clock news. He checks his watch. Where is Richard? He should be here, shaking hands, asking the citizens about their future concerns and current problems, and courting their vote.

King hired college students to hand out "Wright for Governor" buttons and flags, and he observes them standing together, chatting, instead of working the voters. He'll mention something to Amanda. As the campaign manager, it's her job to handle these things. Lately, she and Richard seem to be glued at the hip. They should both be here. He's not Scrooge, so he's allowing them some slack tonight since it's Christmas Eve.

Rounding the corner are his wife, daughter, Stan, and tagging behind them, Rusty and Jamie. Seeing them together always lifts his spirits, a true reminder that he's a lucky man. Rita and Gabby both carry shopping bags, so he'll presume that the day waiting for Richard's speech wasn't too much of a hardship.

Minutes later, a black limousine stops and gets the attention of the crowd. King shakes his head, thinking, *A limo? Can't the guy walk two blocks?* The supporters might think this frivolous and could second guess before reaching into their pockets in the future.

The chauffeur opens the back door, and Richard exits, waves to the crowd, and then turns to assist Amanda. Her white fur coat parts, and her sequined silver dress is hiked up, displaying her long legs. She makes no effort to pull the dress down. Even though the mink might be made of faux fur, the campaign center is sure to get angry messages from the animal rights groups. He explicitly remembers sending a memo about this. The couple looks like they're bound for a red-carpet Hollywood event. If Amanda had checked the schedule, she would know this is a sponsored event by a church group; no decent woman would show up to church in that dress. He adds this to his mental list for future campaign appearances and rolls his eyes. He's exhausted by the constant handholding and the couple's disregard for instruction.

Gabby stands next to her daddy, taking everything in. Her artwork is shown on the banner hanging from the pillars, the flags the supporters are waving, and the balloons floating around. Everything displays the word *freedom:* the word for independence, self-determination, and choice. She thinks of these words and applies them to her situation. She's independent of Richard and determined to stick to the decision that his current behavior restricts his involvement in her child's life. She bites the inside of her cheek.

Richard, with Amanda by his side, slowly ascends the stairs to the entrance of city hall. Amanda is shaking hands and working the crowd. Richard, looking dashing as always, follows her lead. When he stops to admire a baby in a young mother's arms, Gabby's heart hurts.

At the top of the stairs, he faces the group and lifts his head proudly, then turns in their direction. Gabby thinks he directs his smile at her, which fuels her anger. The baby kicks, and she reaches for her stomach. Her condition is evident even under her coat.

"Good afternoon. Merry Christmas." Richard is glowing, matching the bright lights of the nearby decorated tree. His voice is strong and reassuring. Gabby would be compelled to vote for him if voting took place today.

The crowd cheers and raises their campaign flags, waving them back and forth as Richard's campaign song plays loudly, bringing the attention from others walking down the streets, enticing them to join the celebration. Richard quiets the group before continuing his speech.

"Welcome, welcome, my dear friends. Christmas has come to the great state of Texas. Look around you. It's been a great year. But I have a plan to make it even better in the years to come. After I am voted governor, and I am in the house," he says as he points down the street toward the Governor's Mansion, "there will be a renewed sense of freedom in Texas." The crowd cheers again. "Freedom from poverty, freedom for choice, freedom for education, and as always here in Texas, freedom of worship, and freedom of speech."

"Our work intensifies with the upcoming new year. How do you like this banner?" He points to the large sign hanging between the two pillars. "Freedom, yes freedom for the people and by the people. With us this afternoon, we have Gabriella King. Gabby, make yourself known. Gabby is a local artist and a personal friend who did a fantastic job designing our campaign banners and pamphlets."

Taken off guard, she's at a loss as to how to respond.

"Gabby, wave to these kind folks. Let's give her a hand. Thank you, Gabby."

She lifts her hand, and bright lights from the cameras turn in her direction, causing her to squint. Amanda might enjoy the limelight, but Gabby chooses to remain in the shadows. *What is he thinking bringing her this unwanted attention?* The crowd claps.

Then, from somewhere behind her, gunshots fire, and Gabby hears the sound of a bullet as it whizzes by. People scream and duck for cover. Chaos prevails as more shots are fired. A force knocks her to the ground, and someone heavy covers her so forcefully that she can't take in a full breath. She wants to scream, but her voice is gone. Panic overtakes reason, and she struggles, certain that she's going to die. Nearby, a woman shrieks, followed by someone wailing. Lying there motionless with fear, she waits, listening for the gunfire to cease. Time passes.

As she catches her breath, she hears Stan's familiar voice. "Sorry, Gab. You okay? I didn't hurt the baby, did I?"

He turns her over. "Gab?" She gasps for air.

"What happened?"

In the surrounding commotion, she hears a woman weeping and

Richard yelling for someone to call 911. On alert, she pushes herself up on her elbows. The scene before her is terrifying. Richard is bending over Amanda. There's blood on her white fur. *Amanda has been shot. Who would do this?*

Stan helps Gabby to her feet, and she accounts for her daddy, Rita, Jamie, and Rusty. "Let's get you out of here. Mother, come with me." He takes Rita's hand, and she looks at King for approval.

"Go with Stan. I'll meet you later." King rushes up the steps toward Richard and Amanda. Sirens blast. Some people dispersed at the start of the rampage, but from the faces that remain, she reads fear mixed with confusion. Stan pulls her along, and she looks over her shoulder, uneasy about leaving her daddy and concerned about Amanda.

An hour later, the family sits around a table at campaign headquarters, sipping coffee, each giving their version of what happened earlier. King arrives to join them, removes his coat, and takes a seat at the head of the table.

"Wayne, thank God you're here." Rita jumps up from her chair and stands behind him.

"It's okay, dear." They kiss, and her embrace shows an unwillingness to let go. "Get me a cup of whatever you're having, and I'll fill you in." He throws his Stetson on the table and runs his fingers through his white hair.

"First, everyone is all right. One of the bullets braised Amanda. She's at the hospital, and the doctors say she'll be fine. The police are getting a statement from her and Richard. We can only guess that this may have been an assassination attempt on Richard. It's too soon to know, but after the investigation, we'll get the whole story."

"Where's Richard?" Rita asks.

"Until we know more about the shooter, he's with the police in a safe place."

"Did they catch the maniac who did this?" Rita asks.

"Rita, I'll answer all of your questions. Please, I need a minute." He places his hand on his chest, then takes a sip of the steaming coffee. "Starting over. No one was killed or seriously injured. Thank God." He makes the sign of the cross. "Thus far, Amanda is the only one who was injured. She's shaken up and reasonably so, but it appears to be a flesh wound. She'll be treated and released. This could have been so much worse.

"The shooter is a homeless vet who's been camping out at city hall. He has post-traumatic stress disorder and has a history with the city police. It could be that the combination of having his space invaded, since he frequently spends the night on these steps and the noise, sent him back to Afghanistan.

After hearing the shots, some college students saw him waving the gun and running. They tackled him and held him down until the police arrived and arrested him. Richard will be in protective custody until the authorities rule out a political motive. I doubt it was truly an assassination attempt, but there's no denying that the bullets were aimed at Richard. Amanda's arm took the hit instead, just a few inches to the right, and it could have hit Richard's chest. We're very lucky."

"What will happen to him, the vet?" Gabby asks as she twirls a lock of her blond hair around her finger.

"He got himself a night in the slammer, and my guess is that they'll slap him with a 72-hour hold and then move him to a psychiatric ward to have him evaluated. Many of these vets seem to slip through the cracks. It's sad. Sometimes it takes something dramatic like this to get them the help they desperately need." He shakes his head. "It's a sad situation. It will be all over the news—not the coverage I wanted for Christmas Eve. According to Amanda, the guy came running from the street, behind where we were all standing. I shudder to think of how devastating this evening could have ended." King covers his face with both hands and sobs.

Immediately, Rita puts her arms around his shoulders and lays her head against his. "But it didn't, and we have been blessed."

Gabby sits and stares in disbelief. Her daddy is so strong, but sitting here now, he seems old and fragile. She closes her eyes and relives the scene outside city hall earlier. She jerks in her seat, reliving the sound of the bullets. Yes, the bullets could have found any one of the King family before hitting Amanda. How close had she come to becoming a victim of this violent act? She hadn't thought to duck because she wasn't sure what was happening. *Could Stan have saved my life and the life of my baby?* Her whole body begins to tremble uncontrollably. Stan reaches over, and she lays her head against his chest.

"It's going to be okay. I won't let anything happen to you."

She believes him.

CHAPTER 38

The radio blasts Christmas songs on their ride home to the ranch, but no one sings along. The shock of the gunfire on the steps of city hall lingers and dampens their holiday spirit. Gabby rests her head on the car's side window. She doesn't believe it is an accident that Rita has claimed the middle seat, separating Gabby and Stan. This gesture piques her curiosity, and she wonders if Rita is privy to the current status of Marie and Stan's relationship.

Back at the main house, Stan gathers wood and kindling to start a fire, Rita turns on the holiday playlist, Gabby puts the tea kettle on the stove, and Jamie sets platters of shrimp and crab on the table, following in the King family tradition of eating seafood on Christmas Eve.

Before dinner, King unlocks the liquor cabinet and opens the GB Cowboy Bourbon. He needs a drink to settle his nerves. He's thankful that no one was seriously injured in the gunman's rampage. Not waiting to serve others, he pours a double shot, chugs it before wiping his eyes, and then looks up as if saying a prayer.

Gabby, feeling his angst, offers a hug. "I'm sorry, Daddy."

"You have nothing to be sorry about. I'm sorry. I'm sorry for putting you in harm's way. You, the baby, everyone, Rita…"

"Shhhh…you had no way of knowing that a crazy man would be there."

"I am responsible for not having proper security. Any one of us could have been killed. Richard could have been killed. I never thought to put a bulletproof vest on him for public appearances, especially ten months before the election."

"Like I said, it was a fluke. No one expects you to have done anything differently. It's not your fault."

"That's kind of you to say, and I appreciate it. I will be more prepared going forward." He looks down at his vibrating phone. "It's Richard. I need to take this." He steps away, answers, and then returns to announce the update to all.

"Richard says that Amanda is doing better and has been released from the hospital. The docs gave her antibiotics and pain meds. They're at the Driscoll with a security guard at the elevator and another outside their room. He's been watching the news, says the shooting is being covered on every station. He thinks he looks good on film. Just like Richard to think of himself." King chuckles. "I wanted coverage. I got more than I bargained for."

The severity of tonight's events opens Gabby's eyes, allowing her to view her daddy objectively. As his daughter, she had thought him indestructible. Thinking over this past year, it was his wisdom and bravery that engineered the plan that helped arrest Drug Lord Lopez, and he's been the driving force behind Richard's political career. Earlier this year, her daddy saved her and gave her hope when she no longer wished to live.

Her heart aches for this mountain of a man as she views the changes. He appears much older; there are numerous creases around his eyes, and his shoulders fold forward. His large knuckles cause his arthritic hands to look deformed. A dull film has now replaced the twinkle that once sparkled in his eyes. There's a frail quality surrounding him that hints of someone tired from working long, hard hours.

She imagines how he must have suffered watching his only daughter waste away in self-pity and grief. She's stunned when looking at photos snapped the day of Brett's funeral—the thin, fragile widow and the sadness gracing the face of the elderly man holding her up. She was so caught up in her own sorrow that she failed to understand the weight he carried, losing a close friend and later fearing that he may lose her as well. At the time, she was oblivious, but tonight and after months of healing, she's thankful for the insight. She loves him that much more.

"You're deep in thought." Stan always seems to read her. He smells of fresh pine that imitates earthy tranquility and has just a touch of smoke scent from starting the fire.

"Yes, I'm thinking of how grateful I am to have my daddy." She clicks her glass of sparkling water on his filled with bourbon. "Merry Christmas, Stan. Thanks for tonight." Remembering Rita's concerns, she adds, "How's Marie? Have you spoken to her? She'll be frantic seeing the gunman on the news."

Stan clears his throat. "I left a voice message when she didn't pick up. She's usually good at checking her phone." He gets his cell out of his pocket. "But she hasn't called back."

"It is Christmas Eve. She's probably busy with her family."

"Probably." He lowers his eyes.

After the seafood buffet and with drinks flowing, the dark mood dissipates as the warm fire takes the chill out of the event downtown, and the conversation gets livelier. The Kings' earlier concerns melt away in the magic that only Christmas can bring.

Later that evening, when retiring for bed, Gabby turns on the 11:00 p.m. news.

A reporter standing on the steps of city hall announces:

At 5:00 p.m. this evening, Brandon Derrick, a twenty-seven-year-old veteran, fired shots into a crowd gathered at city hall. Senator Richard Wright was addressing a group from the Hill Country Protestant Church before their annual reading of the "Christmas Story" from the book of Mark. The suspect, a homeless man, has a long history of post-traumatic stress disorder. He was apprehended and is in custody. Amanda Jason, Wright's campaign manager, was injured in the gunfire. She's been taken to the hospital and treated for minor injuries. The motives of Derrick are still under investigation, although it's believed that Wright was targeted. Wright, who is running for governor, is currently being interviewed by police. We'll have more on this story as it becomes available."

CHAPTER 39

Christmas Day

On Christmas morning, Gabby wakes to the sound of persistent knocking on her door. What could Stan possibly want at this hour? Or is it Daddy? She crawls out of bed and reaches for her heavy bathrobe before stealing a glance at the clock. It's a few minutes after seven. Something must be wrong. She runs her fingers through her hair, and the knocking gets louder. The morning's overcast gray sky is accompanied by a cold breeze, which hits her face as she opens the door.

Standing outside with a heap of Christmas presents in his arms is Richard.

Completely baffled, she asks, "Richard, what are you doing here?"

"Quick, let me in, for God's sake. Hurry." He looks over his shoulder.

"Okay, you don't have to be mean. Merry Christmas," she says, tongue in cheek. She must look a sight.

"I can't be seen here. You know that."

"Oh, yes, how could I forget?" She stands to the side as he comes through the threshold. "Why are you here?"

"I missed you, and it's Christmas." He pecks her on the cheek.

She pulls back. "You missed me?" She stands with her hands on her hips. "Where's Amanda?"

"Last night freaked her out, and she went to have Christmas with her family." He places the gifts on the counter, takes off his coat, and throws it on the nearby chair. "You got any coffee? I sure could use a cup." He opens her refrigerator. "I don't see the cream."

"You woke me up, so I'll have to make some." Had she thought that Richard had changed? Right now, it seems like he thinks the whole world revolves around him. "No cream, just milk. Hope that will do. Give me a few minutes." She rubs her neck and yawns before turning on her Keurig.

"Wow, look how big you are!" His eyes are round.

"Gee, is that a compliment? Yes, a seven-month pregnant woman has a large stomach. If you had been around these past three months or thought to call, it might be less of a shock. Silly of me to think the father should take an interest."

"Gabby, Gabby, don't be like that. It's Christmas. I came all the way out here just to see you." He gives her a hug. She rolls her eyes and resists pushing him away because it is Christmas.

"It's nice that you drove to the ranch, and I doubt it's because you missed me. Let me guess, Amanda left you for her family, and you were all alone and knew that if you came here, you would be wined and dined and treated like a king. Excuse the pun."

"Part of that may be true. Yes, you're right, I was alone, but it's the perfect time to see you. I've been here for many holidays, so nothing is out of the norm that can't be explained."

"Your coffee's done." She pushes the milk carton across the kitchen counter and places another pod in the Keurig for her cup of morning brew. "We can go in the great room and sit by the tree. You can turn the lights on. The plug is on the right."

"Nice tree," he says as she follows behind.

"Stan brought it over and helped decorate it."

He stands looking out the window. "I've missed the ranch. I love the calmness. Driving here was the quietest time I've had in months." He turns to look at her. "Lately, it's been crazy. Not just the shooting yesterday, which was horrible, and I'm not making light of it, but the entire schedule. King has me at business luncheons daily to generate campaign funds. I'm in Houston for lunch and then driving to Fort Worth for dinner. Sometimes I forget where I am, waking up in one hotel after another. It's rough." He takes a sip of his coffee. "In January, I'm hitting El Paso and then going north to Lubbock. There are so many names and faces, and remembering all of them is a nightmare. I have a stack of three-by-five cards a foot high. And I've got ten more months of this craziness. It's wearing on me. I need a vacation." He pauses, then turns to face her. "I told your father that I needed a vacation, and he said that's why he scheduled Corpus Christie and Padre for the spring." He chuckles. "Imagine that. So kind of him."

She doesn't attempt to interrupt, and part of her is feeling empathy for the guy. *What happened to my rage?*

"Amanda's great. She really is. She loves this stuff. Me, I'm not so sure I'm cut out for it. But…I'm in it far too deep to back out now. King would kill me." He rubs his chin and then stares out the window again. "I think about you a lot. I don't expect you to believe that. It's been hard not calling you or being able to see you, have lunch or dinner. You know, stuff like that, stuff that normal couples do. So often, I think I could go back to work at the firm, make a decent living, come home at the end of the day to you and our child."

Her eyes open wide. *What is he saying? Does he mean any of this, or is he feeling sorry for himself? Did having a close encounter with a bullet have this much of an impact? Should she stop him or allow him to ramble?*

Christmas is full of surprises. As she remembers her daddy's slumped shoulders and the tiredness in his face, Richard's words seem to voice these images. This is his dream, and he's talking about throwing it away. Her heart melts as she hears the words of a man who needs rest and encouragement.

She wants to reach out to hug him and tell him he can do this. *Do I dare?* They were together when her daddy first planted the idea of political office in Richard's head. He was so excited, and she was too. She closes her eyes and remembers:

One night in bed together, with her head pressed on his chest, he played with her long blond strands.

"Election night will be great. What band should we book for the party?"

"Don't you think you're getting ahead of yourself? That's years away."

He turned her face up to meet his. "It's going to happen, I know it. You and me in that big white mansion on Colorado Street. We'll stand on the balcony and wave to our people."

"Governor Wright. It does have a nice ring to it." She giggles.

"It sounds perfect. Governor Wright and Mrs. Wright."

"Is that a marriage proposal?"

"Not yet, but mark my words. It will be. You're going to be there at my side. We can do this, Gabby. We'll do it together."

It was the path they were to forge together, and now, they're apart, and she's having their baby alone. How had their lives gotten so turned around?

She stands next to him, forgoes the hug but rubs his shoulders. "Richard, this is the dream that you've worked years for. This is the home stretch; ten months is nothing. You can do this."

He turns to face her. "Gabby, you're amazing. You're a great listener, level-headed, intelligent, beautiful, classy…what happened to us?"

His eyes are piercing, and it's as though he's trying to look into her soul. Even she's not sure of what he'll find.

Uncomfortable with his stare, she looks away.

"I know I messed up. I got caught up in the power and the prestige. I shouldn't have cheated on you. You would have never gone to Brett if I had been the man you deserved."

"But you did cheat, and I loved Brett. He was…I'm not going to stand here and defend my relationship with my husband, not here in our house." Her eyes flash hurt. "Brett was wonderful. We were wonderful. And now he's gone. How dare you." Her heart is breaking, but her anger keeps the tears from flowing. "Richard, you need to leave."

Richard pulls her into his chest, and she tries to push him away. "I'm sorry. So sorry. I didn't mean for it to come out that way. Please, forgive me." He reaches for her again. "It's Christmas, and I didn't come here to make you cry. I'm sorry. I love you. I don't want to hurt you, please."

She tries not to fall for his antics; however, he had voiced remorse, and his eyes hint at abandonment like a puppy lost out on the street.

He holds her and rocks her. He nuzzles her neck, then lowers his head and kisses her cheek. Taken by surprise, she turns, and he takes the opportunity to find her lips. His kiss is sweet and warm. He's so sad, and she's so sad. She thinks that she should pull away. She still loves her husband. She's still grieving, but Brett is gone, and Richard is here, and he's the father of her child. Still, it feels wrong.

Time spent with Richard is like riding an emotional rollercoaster. Within seconds, she goes from joy to anger and happiness to sadness. It's crazy. Suddenly, her baby kicks, and Richard jumps back, startled.

"The baby has more sense than me. We shouldn't." Her nervous laugh fails to make light of their kiss. However, she wants him to share in their baby's life, so she places his hand on her stomach. "Here, wait, they usually come in a series." After a few seconds, the baby moves again. She watches his facial expression.

His eyes light up. "I felt it. It's like a wave. Is it a boy or a girl?"

"I didn't want to know. I just want it to be born healthy."

"I'm sorry, I should have called before barging in like this. I've had so much on my mind with the campaign."

"Hey, it's okay. We both had a lot going on this past year. How about some breakfast?"

He smiles. "Show me around your kitchen. I'll make the eggs, and you can get out of your pj's. After breakfast, we have gifts to open."

Walking back to her bedroom, she shakes her head. She didn't think Santa would put Richard on her doorstep. Stan, yes, but Richard, the thought had never crossed her mind. Today is going to be interesting.

After the breakfast dishes are done, Richard steers Gabby toward the Christmas tree where he has placed his presents. He guides her to the couch.

"Sit here." He brings over his stack of gifts. From the bottom, he pulls out the biggest one and hands it to her.

"You should open this one first." He sits next to her on the couch and leans forward.

The present is beautifully wrapped. He obviously had it gift wrapped. She tears off the green bow and red wrapping paper and opens the box to a large tan leather Prada bag.

"You can use it as a diaper bag. It's the biggest one the store had." He beams.

"It's very nice. Classy for a diaper bag." She is impressed that he's thought about their baby. "Thank you."

He hands her a second present, wrapped similarly to the first.

"I'm sorry I don't have one here for you."

He frowns.

Seeing his disappointment, she says, "I took all of my gifts over to Daddy's earlier this week. Your gift is under his tree."

His smile returns. This smaller present is a clutch that matches the larger bag.

"Thank you." She opens the zippers, checking the craftsmanship.

Next, he places a third small package on her lap before she finishes inspecting the Prada wallet.

"Richard, why so many?"

"Because I wanted to, and like I said, I've missed you. You're having our baby, my baby. That's pretty special, right?"

"When you put it that way, yes, it is special. However, as special as it is, you're with Amanda. Not me."

He interlocks his fingers. "Gabby, I'm not sure where that relationship is going. Amanda is great in some ways, but we have our problems."

"Sounds normal. Every relationship has problems."

"I can't concentrate on any relationship now. I have the campaign, and that is my life. But I do know that you're going to be the mother of my child. That's a fact, and even though no one in the world can know, it doesn't make it any less so." He pushes her hair back from her face. "Hey, didn't you feel something special when we kissed? You can't deny that." He stares in anticipation that she'll agree. "We're having a baby."

"We shouldn't have. It was wrong." She looks down.

"Only we know what happens here in private. I care for you." He lifts her chin.

"Is that fair to Amanda or to me?"

"I already told you that I don't know what is going on with Amanda."

"Maybe you need to figure that out first."

"First, before what, before starting something here? We're past that, Gabby. Like I said, we're having a baby. Maybe we need to figure out if there is an *us* in the future." He throws his hands up in the air. "The order's all wrong. You get pregnant when your husband is in a coma, the guy who's running for governor is the father, but it's a big secret because the voters won't understand how all of this could happen. And me, the father, can't be a father. We could write a book about this craziness."

"It sucks for me too. I'm doing this all on my own. It would be nice to have you be a part of it." She bites her upper lip.

"It's nasty for both of us. I'm sorry."

"Me too."

"Here, open your last gift. It's Christmas. We need some Christmas joy."

The box looks expensive. She pulls open the bow and lifts the lid. Inside is a channel set square amethyst necklace and matching bracelet. The stones are a gorgeous deep purple. "It's exquisite." She holds the necklace up to the light.

"Let me explain. The baby will be born in February, and the February birthstone is amethyst."

"It's a very thoughtful gift."

"I wanted to give you something that will remind you of our baby and me."

He takes her hand, and after securing the clasp, he rolls the bracelet around on her wrist. Then he holds her hand between both of his and slowly brings it to his lips before placing it on his cheek. "I need you to have a place in my life, Gabby. At this minute, I'm not sure exactly what that place will be. Neither of us knows what the future will bring, but I'll do whatever is best for you and for our child."

His eyes express a deep sadness mixed with sincerity, and she's uncertain about what he's saying, although she doesn't ask him to explain. He rests his head on her chest, and she whispers, "Merry Christmas, Richard. We'll get through this."

CHAPTER 40

Richard places his hand on the small of Gabby's back as they walk through the main ranch house's front door just before noon.

"Merry Christmas," Gabby says as she places the container of chocolate chip cookies on the kitchen counter. Christmas is a favorite King holiday full of traditions: chocolate chip cookies are a must for dessert as much as turkey and brisket are the traditional meats of the meal. Wafts of delicious aroma share the air with Christmas melodies.

Stan, wearing one of his mother's aprons, greets her. "Merry Christmas. I expected you here long before now. I could have picked you up." He leans over to kiss her on the cheek. As he straightens to stand, Richard's presence comes into view.

"Stan, Merry Christmas." Richard holds out his hand.

Stan's jaw drops, and he looks to Gabby as if to say, *what the heck is he doing here?* She lowers her eyes, reading disappointment on his face.

He forces a smile. "Richard, this is a surprise. After last night, we believed you to be stowed away somewhere safe."

"Yes, the police, after speaking with the psychiatrist who assessed Derrick, believe that the noise triggered a psychotic episode. They didn't find anything in his possession or any social media confirming that Derrick was politically motivated. He could not identify me from a photo and denied knowing anything about Richard Wright. It seems he was back in the war. It's sad." Richard rolls his shoulders. "We are extremely lucky that no one was seriously injured. It's a blessing."

"How's Amanda?"

"Amanda's okay. The incident made her realize how short life can be, and she wanted to be with her family. I can't blame her. A few inches to either the left or the right and the outcome would have been very different." He takes off his coat. "I agree with her about family, so I came here. You are as close to family as I have."

Rita comes out of the kitchen. "Yes, you are family. We're glad you're here." She reaches up to kiss him on the cheek. "Merry Christmas. Give me your jacket."

The table is set, and everyone gathers around the marvelous feast before them. King's voice breaks as he says grace, and he stops to wipe his eyes with his napkin. Once again, Gabby is reminded of her daddy's recent vulnerability and wonders if it's a symptom of being overworked or due to his age. Or is there another underlying explanation? Suddenly aware of her nervous habit, she stops twirling her blond strands around her finger.

After grace, they lift their glasses, voicing Christmas cheer, and she forces a smile, determined to keep her worries tucked away for another day.

Another one of Gabby's habits is people watching. Some would call it a hobby. This celebration turns out to be joyous and a day of relaxation packed full of opportunities for people-watching. Gabby observes that Stan's initial coldness to Richard has waned. She has often overheard Amanda's name mentioned in conversation, and she tries to read Richard's expression but comes up short. She also notices that Stan checks his phone frequently and seems distracted.

Richard and her daddy are more relaxed as the hours pass, probably due to the bourbon they have been sampling. Richard gave King a case of different brands, and they have been comparing the notes on their palates. Richard seemed amused after opening her gift, a box filled with books written by former Texas governors, such as Ann Richards, George Bush, and Rick Perry. She told him that he could learn from those who have previously traveled the road.

Jamie plays her role as everyone's mother, and Rita fusses over King. It's pretty typical and as close to normal as they have been as a family since Brett's accident. Everyone seems their usual self. Gabby contemplates how the family sees her. From an outsider's view, is she normal?

Deciding to burn off a few calories from their feast, Jamie and Gabby go for a walk around the ranch. The sun burned off the earlier clouds, and the day turns out to be pleasant with temperatures in the upper sixties. Gabby remembers to put an apple in her pocket as a treat for Lady and some carrots for Brett's horse, Frog. These four-legged beasts are family too.

"It turned out to be a nice Christmas," Jamie says as she pats Frog.

"Better than any of us could have hoped, even with Richard's surprise visit." Gabby turns to the older woman. "I bought flowers for the gravesite. I left them at my house. I've been wanting to see Brett and wish him a Merry Christmas."

"Ah, honey, of course you do." She rubs her arm. You shouldn't go alone. And it gets dark early these days." She turns and walks away.

"Where are you going?"

"I'm going to get Stan."

"Why Stan?" Her brow is furrowed.

She turns and places her hands on her hips. "He's sober. Richard's drunk, and besides that, Richard's a fool."

Gabby detects no glimpse of a smile on Jamie to indicate that she's kidding. Yes, it might be true that today Richard drank too much, but what did she mean by calling him a fool?

Gabby travels down the lane toward her house, listening to the gravel crunch under her boots as she rehearses her lines. How does she say Merry Christmas to her dead husband? She doesn't wish to blubber and fall apart. She wants to be strong, proof that she's moving forward. That would seem normal, right?

"Hey, Gabby, wait up." Stan is donning his jacket as Ryder pulls him along. She slows when she sees his efforts enhance his limp.

"You don't need to run."

"Thanks." He catches his breath and rubs his leg.

She pets Ryder and purposefully looks in another direction because she understands his insecurity when his limp is obvious. The simple act of rubbing his leg reminds her that everyone has a burden to bear.

"Thanks for going with me. I have to stop by the house to get the roses."

"It's good to get some exercise. I ate too much." He rubs his stomach. "Ryder needs his walk, too."

"Were you able to get in touch with Marie? I saw you checking your phone."

"No. I left two messages, and she didn't respond to my texts."

"You seem troubled by that. Want to talk about it?"

"It's Christmas, and I understand that she's with her family. Usually, people who care about each other exchange wishes during a holiday."

"The day isn't over…and there is the time change to consider."

"Guess you're right about the two-hour difference."

They arrive at her drive. "I'll just be a minute." She punches the numbers into her digital lock, which she installed to eliminate the need to carry a key.

While he waits, Stan surveys the house from the roof down to the foundation, making a mental note to whack a few nailheads into the wood on her porch railing.

It's so easy being with Gabby. He enjoys the restful silence. It's refreshing compared to Marie, who tends to chat endlessly. He wonders if that's because she's younger. He tries phoning her for the third time, and like before, he gets her voicemail. She doesn't seem anxious to chat with him today.

In the meantime, Gabby comes out carrying red roses as he tucks his phone back into his pocket.

245

"Ryder, come here, boy. Leave the squirrels for another day." The dog comes to his side.

"Ready?"

"Yep, sorry it took so long. I have this cramping feeling, so I took a few Tums."

"You still want to go to the cemetery?"

"I have to say Merry Christmas to Brett and Jacob. It wouldn't feel right if I didn't. Can you understand?"

"I understand better than you think." He looks at the sun descending on the horizon and thinks of Marie. "We best get moving. It will be dark within the hour."

She takes his elbow, and they walk the rest of the way in silence.

CHAPTER 41

Gabby and Stan return to the ranch house after the cemetery. The men are engrossed in a football game on television, and Rita and Jamie are having tea at the dining room table. The burning fire illuminates the room with a warm glow. Her trip to the cemetery was less emotional than anticipated, but nonetheless, she shivers as if shaking off the coldness of the task. Time does have a way of healing.

She still has an uneasy feeling in her stomach. Maybe it's just her nerves.

"It's been a great Christmas. I'm beat," she says to her family.

"Me too," Stan agrees and gets up from the sofa. "I'll walk with you. I have my flashlight."

"I need to gather my stuff, so give me five, okay?" She exits for the kitchen.

"You got it."

Richard gets up and grabs his jacket. "No need to bother, Stan. I'll walk Gabby home."

Both men stand close as if in a face-off and escorting Gabby is the winner's reward.

"I'll spend the night." Richard grins as he drains his bourbon.

Stan stands back and squares his shoulders as if ready to throw a punch. "I don't think that would be wise."

"And who are you, her keeper?"

"You've hurt her enough already. Besides, you're drunk."

"She's having my baby."

"And you have Amanda, so back off."

"And you have Marie, so back off, buddy." Richard pushes his finger into Stan's chest. "Funny how you see the speck in my eye and cannot see the log in your own. Like I said, back off."

A harsh voice nears, and King separates them. "Stan will walk Gabby home. He's going that way. Richard, you can have the guest room. It's settled." Both men step away. "One would never guess that Christmas is a time of goodwill." King leaves the room.

A deadly silence pervades, and Gabby's people-watching skills send alerts that the two pairs of eyes staring at her indicate that she has been the subject of their disagreement.

She puts her hands on her hips. "I must have missed something. What?"

"Not a thing," Richard says. "Good night, Gab, and… Merry Christmas."

Stan dons his coat and holds out his arm as though their departure is an emergency.

King returns. "Night, Princess." He gives her a kiss and nods to Stan.

Ryder stays close by their side as they walk quickly down the lane to their houses. Gabby's curiosity gets the best of her.

"So, what was going on back there?"

"What?"

"You know what." She pulls on his arm and stops.

"Richard's drunk."

"What did he say? Tell me."

"He wanted to spend the night with you." Stan looks past her shoulder.

"Oh…and?"

"I can't have him hurting you again. He can't have both you and Amanda. It's not fair… to you."

"You told him as much?"

"Damn straight. You're not some cheap tramp." He lowers his voice as if imitating Richard and says, "I'm horny, so I'll spend the night with Gabby. Is that how you got pregnant?"

"Whoa, excuse me. You are out of line."

"Someone needs to protect you."

"Sounds more like a lecture." She puts her hands on her hips and takes a deep breath. "I told you about the low place I was in the day Richard came to the house. So, here's the truth: I was going to kill us both, me and Brett."

Stan stares.

"I don't expect you to understand. You have never been at a place where you don't want to live another day." The words are out of her mouth, and she can't take them back. She remembers just last year when Stan was suffering, self-medicating with alcohol and narcotics after his motorcycle accident. He went to rehab for six weeks. He lives daily with his limp, a constant reminder of the pain. "God, Stan, I'm sorry. It's Christmas."

"I'm sorry too, Gab. I had no idea. I should have been there for you."

"I didn't let anyone be there for me. Okay?" She pulls on his arm and forces their eyes to meet. "It was me, not you. Thanks for looking out for me today. Richard and I have a complicated history. I thought he had changed, and in some ways, he has. Our relationship, or lack thereof, isn't all his fault. There are always two sides to every story, and in this case, there is a third factor to consider, the campaign side with voter reaction."

"Richard is so annoying. Honestly, I can't stand the guy. You deserve better."

"I appreciate your concern. That doesn't change the fact that he is the father of my baby. I have to learn to get along with him for the sake of the child."

"Don't let him play you. That's all I ask. Be smart."

They're at her door. "Thanks for walking me home." She kisses him on the cheek. "I hope you hear from Marie. Give her my best." She pets Ryder. "Merry Christmas to you. Your daddy gives you an extra treat tonight. You're a great dog."

CHAPTER 42

The fire crackles, making the room cozy. Stan props his feet on the hassock with Ryder nestled by his side. He sips a cold beer as he enjoys the Christmas tree's twinkling lights and the soft Christmas music. It's been a long day, and in an hour, another Christmas will be history. He's baffled as to why Marie hasn't made an effort to call. This is their first Christmas, and though they are separated by a thousand miles, he had something special planned for a Facetime call. He holds the small silver package that was to be unwrapped today. He also wants a serious chat about their relationship. Today, her behavior causes him concern about their future together.

He ruminates over Richard's words, that Stan wants both Marie and Gabby. He cringes, knowing there is some truth to this. He despises Richard for openly flaunting his relationship with Amanda, then trying to get close to Gabby. But doesn't he do the same? He shacks up with Marie, though he secretly carries a torch for Gabby. A fire blazes deep inside him whenever he thinks of Gabby and Richard

251

together. As much as he hates to admit it, Richard is right, he is a hyp-ocrite. He glances at his phone. Still no call from Marie.

As Gabby retires for bed, she removes Richard's amethyst necklace and bracelet and holds them between her fingers. The thoughtfulness of this gift came as a surprise. After the awkward start to the day with his unexpected visit, they became quite at ease with one another as the day progressed. Celebrating Christmas together was special after not having any quality time or phone chats for the past several months. She had laughed at his campaign stories and wonders if he purposely avoided mentioning Amanda. In turn, she updated him on the status of her pregnancy and the horse center. Most of the previous ill feelings she carried for him seem to have vanished, and she can imagine them a family…maybe someday.

After placing the matching purple stone set in her jewelry box and closing the lid, she pats the box tenderly as though it contains a living treasure. With the new year only a week away, she resolves to foster a healthier relationship with Richard. New Year's Day is a reason to start fresh, and that's what she is going to do.

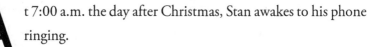

Chapter 43

At 7:00 a.m. the day after Christmas, Stan awakes to his phone ringing.

"Hey, you up?" Marie's voice is cheery.

He rolls over and yawns. "What time is it?"

"It's morning, your time. I thought you were an early riser."

"I usually am. However, I was up late waiting to Facetime with my girlfriend on Christmas. I wanted to open gifts."

"Oh, that's sweet."

"It would have been, but you didn't call me back. Maybe I'll keep my present for next year."

"I'm really sorry. We didn't have a set time or anything. I thought that we would both be tied up with family stuff."

"It would have been nice to say Merry Christmas to each other."

"I said I was sorry."

He chooses to ignore her defensive tone. "So, tell me about your

Christmas." He gets out of bed and opens the curtains to check the weather.

"It was great being home with my family. My brother and his girlfriend drove down from Frisco. Last night, we went to a party. One of his old high school friends hired a band, and the music was pretty loud. I didn't hear my phone ring. We danced until the wee hours of the morning, and everyone got pretty smashed. Then, I helped make breakfast to sober folks up so they could drive home. I haven't been to that wild of a party in a long time. I just got home."

Stan calculates that it's five in the morning, California time. "Did you enjoy it?"

"It was pretty awesome. Yeah, I liked seeing old friends."

"It must be pretty boring for you here on the ranch."

"We should go into town more. Hang out, you know, hit the bars."

"I see."

"I'm not complaining or anything. I'm just saying that it would be fun. Stan, can we talk later? I need to crash. My bed is calling me. Okay?"

"Sure thing, get some rest. Call me later."

The phone is disconnected. He had had concerns earlier about their age difference, and this conversation validates them.

CHAPTER 44

January

"Stan, can you do something for me?"

"Sure, Gab, what do you need?"

"Don't panic or anything, but I think I'm in labor."

"The baby's not due until February. You sure?"

"I thought I was having indigestion, so I took an antacid, but that was hours ago. The cramping is getting worse, and it's at regular intervals. Not close, like two minutes, but still regular." She holds her stomach. "Rita and Daddy are in town, and I don't think I should drive."

"No, no, definitely not. I'll tell Marie, and then I'll be there in a jiff." He checks his watch. It's 8:00 p.m.

Minutes later, Stan is in Gabby's driveway. He runs around the truck, opens her door, and takes her overnight bag.

She smiles. "Thanks. I really appreciate this." She settles into the front seat. "It's not a short drive. I thought Marie might tag along."

"Marie, no. She wishes you well. She knows that babies aren't predictable and that this could turn into a twenty-four-hour shift…or more. I hope for your sake it's not."

"Maybe it's nothing. But it sure feels like something." She gives a small gasp as another wave of cramping starts. "My water hasn't broken."

He pats her hand. "It's better to be safe. I'm glad we're getting it checked out. Did you call your doctor?"

"First thing."

"Good. We should be at the hospital in a little over an hour. I could drive faster."

"There's no need. Let's get there in one piece." She laughs. "Maybe it's just something I ate. I still have a month until the due date."

He blows out a long breath that causes her to hold hers in. He's tapping his fingers on the steering wheel.

"Stan, there's nothing to be nervous about. Everything will be fine."

"Shouldn't I be the one reassuring you?"

She laughs out loud. "I'm not the one with sweat running down my face."

He wipes his forehead with his arm.

She laughs again. "Just kidding. But you are jittery. Take some deep breaths and relax. You'll wear yourself out before we even get there."

At the hospital emergency door, Stan checks Gabby in before parking the car. When he returns, she has already been taken up to the obstetrics floor. He tells a small fib to the nurse on duty. She congratulates him as she escorts him to Gabby's room.

Gabby's in the hospital bed and attached to a fetal monitor.

"How are you doing? Don't blow my cover, but I told them I was the father, so they let me in."

"Okay, Dad, thanks for the warning. It's a good thing we came. Apparently, I'm definitely in labor. The nurse has instructions to phone my doctor when the contractions get closer, and she'll come in to deliver the baby." She rubs her neck. "I can't believe that this is it. I'm having a baby."

"I hope there's a baby, or you would be the first woman in the *Guinness Book of Records* to deliver a basketball." He gives a nervous laugh.

"Should I call my mother and your dad?"

"Sure, but wait another hour since they're at a campaign function. Don't alarm them. Tell them I'm only two centimeters dilated, and this could be an all-nighter."

"Is there anyone else I should notify?"

"You can tell Marie. I'll phone Richard."

His smile fades at the mention of the latter, the man who has the rightful role of the one Stan is imitating. However, Richard has been banned from being at Gabby's side, and he's currently at a campaign dinner with the Kings and, of course, Amanda.

The nurse gives Stan a gown. Gabby laughs as he ducks his head into the room.

"I need a pic of this." She snaps a photo. "This is blackmail material."

He gets out his phone and does the same.

"You delete that."

"Nope, not unless we trade—a delete for a delete."

"Ooh, ouch…" She holds her stomach.

Several hours have come and gone, and the once calm mother-to-be is feeling the effects of labor.

"Gabby, breathe, slowly exhale. Here, squeeze my hand." Stan's coaching makes it almost seem like he's done this before.

The nurse enters. "That's right. Great job, Dad." She glances at the monitors, then says, I think it's time for a cervix check. Let's see how you've progressed."

"Should I leave?" he asks with skeptical eyes.

"No, you can stay, but keep your eyes on mine and put that phone away."

"Yes, ma'am," he says, tucking the phone in his pocket. "No more pics, promise."

"We're making progress, you're at six centimeters and 75 percent effaced. It'll be another couple of hours." The nurse turns to him. "You've been here for hours. Now's a good time for a break." She leaves their room.

Gabby shifts her weight in the bed. "Go get some fresh air, maybe a snack. Just because I can't have anything to eat doesn't mean that you can't." She shoos him away. "Go… get a candy bar and some coffee. I'll read this magazine." She holds up the latest parenting magazine that came in her hospital admission packet. "Go on, get out of here."

"Okay, if you're sure. Don't have the baby while I'm gone."

She crosses her fingers. "Not a chance."

She watches him exit and thinks he's such a nice man. Marie is a lucky lady.

Her phone rings. "Richard, you got my message?"

"You're at the hospital… and in labor?"

"That's right."

"How are you?"

"Doing great. It will be a few hours yet. The contractions come and go, not bad, not yet anyway. How was the campaign dinner?"

"Fine. Truthfully, it was fantastic. We got all the tech companies on board. Steve Prime brought them all in. He's a man of his word."

"That's wonderful news."

"He asked about you. He loves you. Everyone loves you, Gabby. You have this caring air about you, and folks respect that."

"I'll take that as a compliment."

"Of course, it was meant to be. I wish I could be there with you. You shouldn't have to do this by yourself."

"That's nice of you to say. Stan drove me to the hospital. He would be here now, but I told him to take a break before the real action starts."

"He's going to be there for the birth?"

"I believe so. I wasn't going to ask him, but it's nice to have someone here to talk with and help me through the contractions."

There is silence.

"Richard, are we still connected?"

"Yeah, oh, sorry. I got some texts, so I'd better go. Keep me updated."

"Will do."

He's quick to disconnect.

Down in the cafeteria, Stan dials Marie's phone. "Hi there."

"Gabby was admitted?"

"That's right. She's in labor. They say it could take a while."

"Great. You can come home. We're supposed to go out tonight, remember?"

"Oh, I forgot." He rubs his chin. "Marie, I'll need a raincheck."

There's silence from her end.

He feels he must explain. "I can't leave her here alone."

"Rita can be with her. You called them, right?"

"Yes, but they were at a campaign dinner."

"The dinner should be over. You said the baby isn't coming for a few more hours. We have plans. The band that's playing down at the tavern really rocks it." Another long pause. "I should be your priority, not Gabby. What's going on, Stan?"

"What do you mean? It's not like I planned this to ruin our evening."

"She's not your responsibility. She has her dad and Rita. Are you in the room with her?"

"I'm down in the cafeteria."

"Were you in the room with her? Holding her hand?"

"I'm not going to lie to you. Yeah, that's what a friend would do."

"A friend."

"Yes, a friend. You're with her while I sit here alone…when we had plans to go out. I got a new dress and shoes. We hardly ever go out."

"Sounds a little like how I felt at Christmas waiting for you to call."

"You're punishing me."

"No, I would be there if I could."

"That's just it, Stan. You're choosing to stay at the hospital with Gabby. I'm going to listen to the band. If you change your mind, you know where I am."

"Marie…" There's only silence. He shakes his head.

CHAPTER 45

After eighteen hours in labor, Gabby looks into the face of her precious baby boy. He's warm and pink, and he squints in the bright light. She counts his fingers and his toes. He's perfect. She holds him tight and kisses his head full of dark hair. He weighed in at six pounds, seven ounces, and measured twenty inches long. She smiles as joyful tears collect in her eyes. This gift has been her lifeline during this past year of tragedy. It's something short of a miracle that Richard arrived at her door that summer's eve and that she conceived this dear savior. She's sorry that with their present circumstances, Richard missed the birth. Her eyes lift to view the man who was by her side during this absolute miracle.

"He's pretty amazing. Wow, what an experience. You did really well. Thanks for sharing this. I'll always remember." Stan nods his head. "It was special."

The nurse comes to take the baby away but promises to bring him back shortly.

"Thanks. I'll remember that you were here for me. I'm sorry to have caused a fight between you and Marie. Tonight, take her out for a nice dinner and maybe a little stargazing. It worked before; it can work again." She winks.

"I hope you're right. She isn't answering my calls." He looks out of the window. "I wonder what time she got home—probably in the wee hours of the morning. Our twelve-year age difference is causing problems."

"You'll work it out. It's a little bump in the road. You make a great couple."

CHAPTER 46

March

Six weeks have passed since her son's birth. Gabby rocks on the porch with her shoulders draped in a blanket. The dreary days of winter give way to signs of spring as the trees bud, and the blue hue of bluebonnets blanket the meadows. She has had several brief phone conversations with Richard since leaving the hospital, and regularly she sends him pics of the baby, but it's disappointing that he hasn't made an effort to see his son.

When she watches the news, they often cover his travels to cities and towns across the state. Her daddy and Rita have been on the campaign trail nearly as much as Richard. King blazes the path, arriving at the towns beforehand to ensure that everything is in order. Routinely, this job would fall under the scope of the campaign manager; however, King leaves the day-to-day details to Amanda since history has shown that Richard accepts the stress of an overly busy schedule better under her direction. The hard work seems to be paying off because the endorsements are coming in, and the polls are favorable.

Gabby has never seen her daddy more focused or wanting anything as much as he seems to want Richard as the next Texas Governor. She's sure Rita encourages King to travel since Rita enjoys the excitement of the shopping, entertainment, and restaurant choices the different cities offer. Almost daily, a package arrives with another outfit or toy for the new grandson from their adventures. Most of these parcels contain a handwritten note that mentions Richard, such as: "Richard sends a hug to Matthew" or "Tell Matthew 'Hello' from Richard." Gabby doubts if Richard has a clue about the notes, and she feels Rita does this on her own.

She loves being a mother, and with the busy infant schedule, she cherishes these times when she can sit on the porch and relax. Minutes later, a cry sounds from the baby monitor, signaling her that Matthew has awakened from his nap.

CHAPTER 47

"Marie, you look beautiful tonight." The candle from the table flickers, highlighting her face. Her long dark hair shines, and although she's dressed in a low-cut navy dress that shows cleavage, Stan thinks she looks young. He fingers the small box in his right suit pocket. This is his moment. He was going to propose on Christmas day, but when Marie failed to call, he didn't have the opportunity. Then he considered New Year's Eve, but as the night progressed and the alcohol flowed, he changed his mind. Now for a third time, he's nervous and uncertain. Some would call this "having cold feet" and that it is perfectly normal when entertaining a major life decision.

"Are you feeling okay?" Marie reaches her hands across the table.

"Yes."

"You seem lost in thought."

"Sorry."

He's saved by the waiter, who comes with a bottle of champagne and pops the cork, then pours two glasses. He gives the cork to Stan.

"Are we celebrating? I don't understand."

Stan hands one of the champagne flutes to her and says, "Marie, I love you."

She doesn't respond.

He waits a few seconds, then says, "I propose a toast to us." He wishes she would say something to help ease his apprehension.

He places the box on the table and pushes it in front of her.

"This was your Christmas present."

"Is this what I think it is?"

"Open it."

"I'm not sure I want to."

His jaw falls open. Beads of sweat break out on his forehead, and his stomach drops.

With shaky fingers, she pulls on the ribbon and opens the box. Her hand goes to her chest. "It's beautiful." She lifts out a silver ring with a large square diamond.

He kneels next to her chair and reaches for her hand. "Marie, will you marry me?"

He sees her watery eyes and follows a tear as it drips off her chin.

"I'm sorry. I can't. Please get up." She wipes her eyes with her napkin. "You're a great guy, and you may be *my* guy, but it's not the right time for us. I was going to tell you that…" She takes a breath. "I'm moving out. I signed a lease earlier this week on an apartment. In the past few months, I've learned that I'm too fragile to make a commitment. When we met, I was vulnerable. I had been through a horrific experience. I almost died. You were my savior, my hero, and I am forever grateful."

Stan opens his mouth to protest. She covers his lips with her hand.

"Hear me out. I need to find out who I am. We can still date, see each other. I'm not saying that I want to break up or that I want to date other guys. I'm saying that I need to step back. We happened too fast. It would be unfair to you and me if I accepted this ring."

He shakes his head. "Wow."

"Take a moment to think about the past few months. We've been fighting. We disagree on many things. You want to stay home, and I want to go out. You like eighties music, and I like what's hip now. And then there's Gabby…I feel like you would pick her over me. Time after time, for whatever reason, whenever she calls, you drop everything and go to her. I count, Stan. My feelings are important. I feel like I am second best."

"You're right."

She sits up straight in her chair, her eyes wild.

"You're right," he repeats. "Call it maturity or wisdom, but I'm not going to sit here and convince you. Picking a life partner should be a joyous occasion, and if you need convincing, then you're right; it's not the right time." He takes the ring from her hand, returns it to the box, and puts it back in his pocket.

"That's it." She waves her hands in the air.

"Yes, so tell me about the apartment you rented."

"You're kidding, right?" She leans forward, her elbows on the table.

"No, we've shifted direction. Instead of making plans for us, we're talking as if we're dating, you know, friends. I thought that was what you were saying. Have I gotten it wrong?"

"You should be upset. I don't understand."

"I am upset. Clearly, any guy would be. I'm certain of what I want."

"You expect us to have dinner now, like none of this ever happened?"

"Pretty much." He drains his glass of champagne. "Good stuff." He pours himself another. "You haven't touched yours."

"I can't do this." She stands.

"Do you want me to call you a cab or drive you home or to your apartment or whatever?"

"You're impossible." She chokes back more tears.

He can't tell if she's angry or confused. "Marie, sit down. Let's talk about it." He reaches out for her hand. "Tell me why you're so upset. What's going on?"

She takes a tissue from her purse and wipes her eyes.

His heart aches for both of them. "I understand that you're young, and at your age, I had no idea what I was doing or where I was going. I get it. Like you said, you've been through a lot. I like us. I thought you liked us too, so I thought, why wait? The human trafficking and Brett's accident are clear signs that reveal how short life can be. I thought we were happy. I thought you were happy." He plays with his fork. "I want to move forward, and I thought we could move forward together. However, if you're not ready, then it would be a mistake, a huge mistake we would both end up regretting." He looks into her face and can see that she's somewhat calmer.

"Once again, you're right. I'm sorry." She sniffs and nods her head. "Can we talk about Gabby?"

"She's my stepsister and has been through a horrific year. She was very fragile there for a while. Having the baby seems to have given her a purpose. I don't worry about her as much." He holds her face in his hand. "I love you, and I'm sorry. Okay? I can wait. I'll still be here, and when you're ready, you let me know."

She smiles. "I do love you."

He kisses her hand. "I'm glad. Are we okay?"

"Yeah, we're fine."

"Good." He pushes his chair back to leave.

"Stan, let's stay and have dinner."

He raises his eyes. "You changed your mind?"

"Please." She reaches for him. "I'd die if you weren't in my life."

"I'm hungry, and we're already here. It's one of the best restaurants—took me two months to get a reservation."

"We can't let the champagne go to waste." She lifts her glass.

"That would be a crime." He pulls his chair in. "The restaurant is known for their escargot. Should we share an order?"

She lifts her glass to click his. "Sounds divine." Then, she leans over and kisses him. "Thanks for understanding and giving me time." She smiles. "You're a great man."

"I'll look forward to the day when you say yes."

CHAPTER 48

March

Gabby stands and waves to the crowd gathered at the Longview Rodeo Arena. She's unsuccessful in faking a smile as she concentrates on the pounding in her chest. When the idea was first presented, she begged her daddy to accept the plaque. King used the argument that Brett's wife is the rightful recipient, and it's her duty to honor her husband. After losing her campaign to sit and observe from the stands, she knows her daddy is correct. She'll need to be strong. However, using this opportunity to advance Richard's political career trumps honoring Brett, which burdens her heart.

Richard will be giving the opening tribute before introducing the president of the Texas Pro Rodeo Circuit's local chapter for the memorial presentation, providing media coverage of Richard and her together. King argues that if she wants to have Richard in their son's life, their public exposure needs to happen gradually, and a ceremony honoring her late husband is the perfect opportunity. She can't decline, but she feels shame using her husband's tribute as a platform for starting her orchestrated romance with Richard—a romance to woo the people by weaving a fairytale and a happily ever after as the dashing white knight saves the bereaved young widow. Richard will be portrayed as a hero.

Richard stands at the podium on the temporary stage, assembled in the middle of the arena, dressed in a red checkered shirt, blue jeans, Stetson hat, and newly purchased red leather boots, displaying a more casual appearance than his usual suit and tie. He gives the opening address, then turns the program over to the President of the Texas Pro Rodeo Circuit.

"Welcome. It is my pleasure to give tribute to Brett Matthews. Quoting Tracy Byrd, 'Rodeo ain't no ordinary life, but a cowboy ain't no ordinary man.' Brett Matthews was an extraordinary man." The lights dim, and all turn their attention to the images on the jumbo screen. The video, accompanied by Western music, displays photos of Brett and clips of his rodeo tour performances. The video concludes with a list of his accomplishments and shows Brett holding the belt he won in Vegas. The crowd cheers.

Fighting back the tears, Gabby is reminded of the man she continues to love and the current dark void she faces. Although she takes pride in knowing that his contribution to the sport is being recognized, her legs are weak. Her daddy's arm tightens around her to give her support. Slowly, he guides her to the podium so the circuit president can hand them the plaque. Following the president's lead, Richard shakes King's hand, then pulls Gabby in for a hug.

Richard whispers, "I know this is hard. You're doing great."

He lifts her hand above their heads and faces forward. The crowd stands in applause. The flash from the cameras resembles a strobe light, and the noise is deafening. Fearing collapse, she tells herself to breathe. Their raised arms form the *V* for victory. The fairytale begins.

Back in her seat as she watches the rodeo, she can't remember walking off the stage. She sits between Richard and her daddy, the plaque in her lap. She reads the inscription:

In Memoriam
Brett M. Matthews
To honor his support and contribution to rodeo
with much appreciation and gratitude.
Presented by
The Texas Pro Rodeo Circuit

As she is leaving the arena, a cowboy stands at the end of her row. Maybe she's being paranoid, but it seems as if his eyes offer a challenge. He tips his Stetson, and it's as though he's waiting for some kind of an acknowledgment. There is something oddly familiar about the stranger. It leaves an unsettled feeling in her stomach. Have they met?

275

CHAPTER 49

King asked the family to meet at his downtown condo since today is the culmination of their hard work on the campaign. If this first milestone is achieved, their end goal becomes a brighter reality. However, today's primary election is not the reason for her excitement. It is because, for the first time, Richard will meet his son.

Over the past two months, they have had Facetime calls but always from King's office so that the calls look like a grandfather checking in with his daughter about his grandson. Sometimes she thinks her daddy is overly protective, and it angers her that Richard has been kept from his son. But her daddy insists that the timing isn't right and that her relationship with Richard needs more cultivation.

Gabby paces the length of the condo with Matthew asleep in her arms. Her son is nearly two months old. She's happy that he is napping because she wants him at his best later. The sleeping baby has his father's nose and his dark hair. She's waited for today, the first time Richard will hold his son and peer into his eyes. He'll be able to feel his silky skin and smell the soft scent of baby lotion. She hopes he will form a connection that will lead to a loving, bonding relationship. She's giddy with anticipation as she opens the curtain to check the driveway for her daddy's car.

Stan is the first to arrive. She opens the door before he knocks and holds her finger to her lips.

"Let me put him down in his crib," she says, then returns. "Hi! Where's Marie?"

"She really likes this campaign stuff. Last I saw her, she was parading a 'Wright for Governor' sign up and down the pavement at the college." He rolls his eyes. "I'm getting tired of all of this."

"If you are, think of what it is like for Daddy. I can't even begin to imagine. If Richard wins the primary, we'll have seven more months of this. Better get used to it. The polls have him winning by 76 percent."

"You should hear Marie talk about him. It's Richard this and Richard that. One would think he walks on water." He opens the refrigerator.

"Sounds like you're jealous."

He twists the cap from the beer bottle and takes a swig. "Maybe. Both you and I know he's not that great."

She bites her lip. She has vowed not to speak ill of her baby's father.

"He's selfish, and..." Stan is interrupted by King and Rita entering.

"How's it going?" Gabby asks, eager to change the subject.

Rita flops down on the couch. "I'm exhausted. If he wins tonight, I'll be too tired to celebrate."

"That's *when* he wins, Rita, not *if*," King is quick to add as he rubs his wife's shoulders.

"Where's my dear little grandson?"

"He's taking a nap," Gabby says.

"I should be doing the same. Been on my feet all day. They're killing me." Rita flings off her shoes.

Stan asks, "Marie didn't come with you?"

"No, child, we left her with Richard. Oh, to be young and have all of that energy." She rubs her feet.

Stan frowns, clearly unhappy.

King turns on the television. "It's almost time for the five o'clock news. Let's see how our boy is doing."

Rita serves a platter of cheese with wheat crackers to hold them over until dinner, and all eyes are glued on the numbers flashing across the large screen.

Shortly thereafter, laughter interrupts their TV viewing, and the door bursts open. Richard and Marie are evidently sharing a private joke.

"Here's the man of the hour," King says, and he stands to greet them.

Richard grins and ushers Marie to a chair opposite Stan. The group shares stories of their day dealing with folks outside voting stations. Gabby watches how Richard's eyes gleam, and she's patient, waiting for him to give her a sign that he knows she's in the room or ask about his son.

After listening to campaign talk for half an hour, she quietly leaves the room to check on Matthew.

She jumps when he first touches her, then wraps his arms around her waist and rests his chin on her shoulders as their eyes land on the peacefully sleeping baby.

"He's so special. We made a beautiful baby." Richard nuzzles her neck, and his warm breath raises goose bumps on her arms.

"He is wonderful. I feel so blessed. I've waited a long time for you to hold your son."

"You understand that I would be with you if I could."

She remains quiet. He turns her to face him. "You know that, right?"

Unable to face him, she turns and steps back, but the wall keeps her close. She chews her upper lip.

"Gabby…" He narrows the gap between them, lifts her chin, and stares into her eyes. "You didn't answer."

She turns away, but he's insistent, waiting until she faces him again.

"Don't," she says. He's so close she feels his breath on her cheek.

"Why not?" He wipes her tear, holds her cheek in his hand. His lips brush hers as if teasing. "I've missed you," he whispers. This time his kiss is more passionate. She presses harder against the wall. She's trapped. Why is she allowing him to manipulate her? He has Amanda.

"Gabby, look at me."

She can't be hurt again. They have to work together for the sake of their child, but…

"God, I've missed you." He buries his face in her hair. "Believe me, I would be with you and our child if I could."

He's saying all of the right things. Is it an act? Can he be trusted? Matthew needs his father in his life. She deserves better than being his dirty little secret. If he's playing a game, the stakes are high. His hand slips between her legs.

"I want you," his breathless voice says. He presses tighter, and he's aroused.

"Stop, we can't. I can't."

"But we can," he whispers in her ear. "The door's closed. No one will know."

"I'll know, Richard."

"Come on, Gabby, stop with that hard-to-get act. You want this as much as I do. Or are you too proud to admit that we have something here? We've made a baby."

She is reminded of Stan's cutting words, that Richard's conduct implies that she is a "cheap tramp." "What do we have? You're still with Amanda."

"It's the optics. Of course, she's my campaign manager. Today is our biggest day. I can't break up with her. That doesn't mean I love her."

"You can't have us both." She straightens her dress.

"You're acting like a child."

"You say that whenever we disagree." She is furious that she's once again riding the rollercoaster of emotions that Richard brings.

Today was supposed to be special. She opens the door to leave then runs into Stan in the hallway.

"Hey, what's going on? You seem upset. What did he say?"

She puts on her poker face. "Nothing. It's nothing." She pushes past him. Did he notice that her face is flushed?

Minutes later, Richard exits with Matthew in his arms. "Look who woke up from his nap."

Gabby scrutinizes to see if he's supporting Matthew's head properly. She doubts if he knows anything about the care of a newborn. She smiles because he's trying, even though he seems nervous. Her phone camera clicks. She's waited months to snap a photo of Matthew with his dad. It's a step in the right direction.

The doorbell rings. Rita goes to answer.

"I have an envelope for Gabriella King." Rita reaches out to take it. "Are you Gabriella?"

She shakes her head.

"Sorry, ma'am. I need Ms. King to sign."

Gabby stands behind Rita. "What's going on?"

"He needs you to sign for this letter."

She creases her forehead and signs her name.

Opening the envelope, she says, "I don't understand. A claim has been filed to dispute the estate of Brett M. Matthews."

"By whom?" Rita asks.

"It says by a Brandon Matthews." Gabby's voice is faint, as though she is thinking out loud. "I don't recall Brett mentioning any family."

"Neither do I. Surely he would have said something," Rita says.

King flips his hand in the air. "It could be someone with the same last name who read the obituary and wants a piece of the inheritance. I wouldn't worry about it." Her Daddy gives her a reassuring look. "Hand me the letter. I'll take care of it.

"Now, let me see my grandson." He laughs jovially, and the tension that had filled the room dissolves.

Together in the condo, they watch the primary results. Instead of going out to a restaurant, they order pizza. The more the results show Richard winning, the more relaxed the family becomes. Richard sits on the floor next to her, and the earlier scene in the nursery flashes in her mind. Though Stan and Marie are kind to each other, she detects that something's amiss. Does everyone have relationship troubles?

When Amanda arrives, the atmosphere of the previous family gathering changes, and the condo becomes like campaign headquarters. The conversation is business oriented as the precinct results are announced.

Gabby feels her blood pressure rise whenever Amanda touches Richard, and his facial expressions imply that he's open to these advances. Did he not just plead his case to be with her? It's as though he wants them both. She makes a tight fist, recalling how the crowd cheered as Richard pulled Amanda up on stage back in October when he announced his run for governor. Will tonight be a repeat? She's been through too much for games, and she has her son to consider.

With 90 percent of the count in, at 10:00 p.m., they are ready for Richard's acceptance speech and the celebration party. King beams, and Richard seems happier than Gabby has ever seen him. Amanda is ecstatic.

King looks to his daughter. "Coming?"

"I'm going to stay here with my son and watch on the television. Congratulations. You worked hard for this. Enjoy."

"You sure? He's in good hands here with Rita. This could be a great opportunity."

She hates that he looks disappointed. "Go have fun." She nods. "Congratulations, Richard."

CHAPTER 50

July

The sun is shining, and the Texas heat is intense, just like it was the day her love left this earth. It is one year later, and she has survived. With a gambler's mindset, she recognizes that back then, the odds had been stacked against her standing here today. With that thought, her eyes lower to the small face in the baby carriage. This baby is her savior.

Matthew, now six months old, is a happy child, and he favors the King side of the family. Although on close inspection, one might see Richard's mouth. She cherishes this bundle and thanks God every day. In his chubby little hand, he firmly grips the carved wooden horse from Veteran Gregg. Choosing the horse as his favorite toy gives her comfort, and she wonders if Brett somehow places the toy in Matthew's hand.

Visiting the family cemetery and standing at Brett's grave, she looks up through the branches of the old oak trees to the blue sky and says a silent prayer: *I still miss you, and I'll always love you.* She believes God sent Richard that evening in May to prevent her from carrying out her plans to end their misery. God extended His mercy when he ended Brett's suffering, then gave her Matthew, so she didn't have to face the future alone. She knows that healing does come with time.

King places his arm through his daughter's. "Are you okay? You're pretty quiet."

"I miss him."

"I know. I miss him, too. He was happiest out riding the pastures on Frog. That boy loved the ranch, and he loved you." He pulls her closer. "He'll always be with us."

King places the potted daisies at the headstone, then picks up the coins that have been left on the grave and hands them to her. "Others remember our fine cowboy, too."

"I miss his green eyes and his dimple." She rolls the coins in her hand.

"The wranglers tell stories about him daily. He was one of a kind." He reaches in his pocket. "I want to give you something."

After gently opening her hand, he places the red threaded bracelet with the gold knot and covers it with his hand. In his wisdom a year ago, he kept the treasured bracelet he had found tossed on Brett's hospital bed.

"Hear me out. The bracelet didn't deceive you. I know you believe that it did. The bracelet's meaning was for good relationships and for good fate. Your relationship with Brett was special. Many people are never blessed with that kind of love. But he said relationships, *plural,* and you have more life to live. So, that's only half of the bracelet's meaning. There's the part about good fate. It's your bracelet and your fate, not Brett's fate. The monk gave it to you. He blessed you."

She searches her daddy's face with wide eyes.

He squeezes her hand. "You and Richard have a son. That is a bond that should be nurtured. Richard needs you, Gabby. Take advice from a wise old man who sees the big picture. Stand by Richard. Years ago, you both had a dream. Believe in that dream, and turn it into a reality." He touches her cheek. "I love you, Princess. The past year has been tough. Put it in the past. The family you always wanted waits for you. Your son needs his father."

The sincerity on his face melts her heart. He wants this so badly, but does she want the same?

"Take the bracelet. Think about it—good relationships and good fate."

CHAPTER 51

September

As the summer turns to fall, Gabby contemplates her father's words daily, turning them over in her mind to gain perspective on her life. Also, seeing her son grow gives her encouragement and creates a magic that reminds her to watch for small miracles every day to find love and God.

With this hope for the future, at some point, she'll stop looking back. Brett was her soulmate, and she'll carry him in her heart forever. But she's a King, and Kings are known for their strength, so she pushes forward, one small step each day.

She twirls the gold knot on the True Lover's Knot bracelet around her wrist. It catches the sun and glistens like a treasure. If she decides to make a life with Richard, will the bracelet's meaning hold true? Her daddy's wisdom speaks of a future to embrace with this man. It's her choice, her freedom to choose the purpose of her life. If she chooses a relationship with Richard, she'll be entwined with the people of Texas, like the threads that form the knot on the bracelet. If she believes the knot represents her destiny, does she have enough strength for this journey?

On a warm evening a week later, the King family attends a political forum downtown. They're greeted at the door by Edward Smith, editor of *Capital Magazine,* who will be on stage with Richard moderating tonight's event. Amanda stands by Mr. Smith, looking professional in her blue tailored suit and heels and carrying a clipboard. The venue seats three hundred-fifty guests, and a full house is expected. Banners displaying Gabby's artwork hang over the doorway.

"Mr. Smith, it's so good to see you again. You've met my wife, Rita, and this is my daughter, Gabby."

He turns toward her and extends his hand. "I've heard wonderful things. It's good to put a face to the name."

His handshake is firm but polite as their eyes make contact.

"Likewise. I read your monthly magazine. I loved the article featuring our horse center. The photography was amazing. Thank you for the exposure. When the veterans read their interviews, it really lifted their spirits. I wished you could have seen the pride on their faces."

His eyes light up, and her daddy stands straighter, proud of his daughter's wisdom in complimenting the man who will later set the tone on the stage.

King focuses on Amanda, who is busy writing notes. "Everything good to go?"

She nods. "We're ready. Richard's meeting with the press now." She checks the time on her cell.

King turns his attention back to Smith. "Be nice to our boy tonight."

Smith chuckles. "I look at these forums as tests. The governor has tough decisions to make. Let's see if he holds up under pressure."

"He'll pass with high marks," Amanda is quick to respond.

Smith pats King on the shoulder. "Worried like a dad for his son. Sit back, relax, enjoy the show." He ushers them to the front row, roped off with tape. "I hope these seats meet your expectations. We'll talk at the gathering after. Enjoy."

The music is loud, and the lights flash to announce the start of tonight's political event. Richard enters from the back of the auditorium, and as he advances down the aisle, he greets citizens with handshakes and hugs friends. He's rather dashing, looking every part the man ready for the office he seeks. Gabby is quick to notice that his tie is made with a print of her artwork. His outward display of appreciation for her work gives her pride.

As he approaches their row, King stands and whispers in his ear. Gabby observes that the two men seem to have cemented a close and more intimate bond, different from their interactions with one another at the condo the night of the primary. Richard nods in her direction before approaching the stage, and he reflects her smile. From this momentary exchange, her heart beats slightly faster.

After introductions, the forum starts. Smith fires questions at a steady pace, as if wishing to squeeze as much as possible into their limited block of time. Richard seems composed, but at times, he taps his foot. This is an outward sign of anxiety, a habit she noticed when they first met.

She recalls their conversation nine months ago, at her house on Christmas morning. Richard confessed he wanted them to be together as a family. She reaches for the amethyst hanging from her neck and moves it back and forth. She smiles, reminded that like Richard, who taps his foot when he's nervous, she reaches for a necklace or twirls a strand of hair.

She does feel a connection with him, but it's unlike the love she had for Brett. It's more like a shared union, and she wonders if the desire to reach for common goals is enough to get them through hard times. Glancing at her daddy, she notes that he seems totally engrossed. She understands because he has invested both money and years of his life to get Richard into the white mansion adjacent to the capitol.

Richard was handpicked for this mission, and he is on the last lap of the campaign, edging his way to the finish line. King has always been a good judge of character, and she prays that Richard will do the work of the office to the best of his ability, proving that her daddy has made the right choice.

Her daddy, in his wisdom, has given her the green light. With this same wisdom, he provided an escape for her when she was so tangled in a knot and had no idea of how to get free. Is she strong enough to take on this enormous challenge, or is she getting caught up in the excitement? As one united front, she and Richard could do some good for the state they both love. Once upon a time, this had been their dream.

Many times since Brett's passing, she has wished to run away from the woman at the ranch, the wife of the rodeo champion. By accepting the challenge to stand by Richard's side, she'd be changing things up and creating a different life. Is that the new life she wants?

The forum lasts about an hour. Under the bright lights, beads of sweat mark Richard's forehead, and she feels his release of tension as he shifts his weight in the chair. After thanking Smith, his campaign song with the theme of freedom plays, and he stands, waving to the crowd.

Back at the ranch, Stan watches the political forum from his couch. The only fault he finds in Richard's performance is his display of arrogance. Otherwise, his responses to the questions were insightful and also offered solutions to problems. He was ready to switch off the television, but his attention spikes when he sees the Kings in the front row. Then he witnesses a scene that crumbles his world. He's stunned, his eyes frozen to the screen as he sees Richard walking off stage, passing Amanda before reaching his hand out to Gabby. What is happening?

Gabby is surprised by Richard's outstretched hand. Her daddy nods at her as if giving approval. *What does this mean?* She hesitates, then accepts Richard's hand. He pulls her out of the row and leads her up the steps onto the stage. They pass Amanda, who wears a scowl, her arms crossed. The audience claps, and suddenly the music gets louder. Richard's bright eyes and wide smile show that he's pleased, and as

Gabby focuses on his mouth, she sees an older version of her son. Her heart skips a beat.

Turning, Richard lifts their clasped hands above their heads as if in a victory sign, like he did before at the rodeo. The crowd cheers louder. He pulls her close for a tight embrace, and she's glad for the support because her knees shake. The deafening sound of the music and the clapping disorients her thoughts. To steady them, she focuses on the audience. Her attention lands first on Steven Prime, who stands giving the thumbs-up sign, and then her heart swells, watching tears roll down her daddy's face. *They seem happy. I'm terrified!*

By accepting Richard's hand and stepping up on the stage, she's stepping out of her comfort zone in the shadows and standing in the light, blinded by the camera flashes. There's a transformation happening as the new replaces the old—*I'm on my way to the Governor's Mansion.* Her smile is genuine. She's made a choice, and at this moment, it feels right.

Acknowledgements

This was an emotional story to write; nonetheless, a story that needs to have a voice.

If you have a caregiver story to share, I would love to listen, so please contact me through my website www.donnaleeoverly.com. As always your review on Amazon and GoodReads, or my webpage are always a blessing.

This book would not have been possible without the help of many others and I am extremely grateful. Thank you to girlfriends who listen and provide insight, the experts who shared their precious knowledge, and my beta readers. I am thankful for Erin Liles, my understanding editor, and Roseanna White, the designer of this beautiful cover and interior.

A special note of thanks to my family for putting up with me: my husband for his continuous love and support of my hobby, and to my son, Dan, for saving my manuscripts (just in case I crash my computer), advice for scene improvements and for his awesome IT skills.

DonnaLee